To Sandy,
I hope you enjoy this
as much as I enjoyed
writing this old friend.
your old friend.

Julie Hodgson

THE
QUIET LIGHT

IN SEARCH OF CAROLINA'S LOST TREASURE—A CARLI OWENS ADVENTURE

GEORGE DICK AND
TALIA HODGSON

iUniverse, Inc.
Bloomington

The Quiet Light
In Search of Carolina's Lost Treasure—a Carli Owens Adventure

iUniverse books may be ordered through booksellers or by contacting:

iUniverse
1663 Liberty Drive
Bloomington, IN 47403
www.iuniverse.com
1-800-Authors (1-800-288-4677)

ISBN: 978-1-4697-4663-0 (sc)
ISBN: 978-1-4697-4664-7 (ebk)

Printed in the United States of America

iUniverse rev. date: 01/25/2012

My name is Carolina Louanne Owens—Carli for short. This is my story. Well it's not exactly my story, although I am in it.

I grew up thinking my Papa's life was kind of boring, only ever puttering away in his woodworking shop building dollhouses for my Granny Sienna, never doing anything of interest or excitement. Never did I imagine that the life he lived long before I came along had been full of adventure. I suppose that's the case with most of us. We only see people as we know them now. We form an opinion until we actually get to know them, listen to their stories, and see what they are really like. We don't know what challenges they had to overcome, what sacrifices they have endured or decisions they made in their past that have created who they are until we delve a little deeper. Of course, never did I think for a moment that my Papa's past would involve hidden treasure, pirates, a secret, underground society in Scotland, the American Revolution, and an unsolved murder in South Carolina.

My earliest memories with my Papa go back to when I was about five years old.

"Papa," I whispered. "It's too dark. Can you snuggle me a bit?"

"Okay Carli—but just for a bit. It's already way past your bedtime."

"Papa, what happened to your dog, Otis? I liked Otis a lot. I miss him."

"I miss him too, he was a good dog. He passed away."

"What's passed away mean?"

"He died."

"Why did he die Papa?"

"Well, he got old. When you get old you eventually die."

"Will I get old Papa? I don't want to die."

"That's a long way off Carli. You're only five years old. You have got a lot of living to do first. Don't be worrying yourself about that."

"Papa, why do boys like girls?"

"Well God made things that way so that boys would be attracted to girls then they would find a person to marry and have children of their own."

"Oh."

"Why do you ask?"

"Well some boys in my class like me."

"I see," Papa smiled. "I don't think that you need to worry about getting married yet. I think those boys just want to be your friends."

"Oh, that's good. Papa?"

"Yes Carli."

"Why do you have hair in your ears?"

"When you get older you start to get hairs in your ears and your nose and you start to lose hair on your head."

"Yuck. How come you were sneezing a lot today Papa? Are you sick? Do you have a cold?"

"No Carli. I have allergies."

"What are allergies?"

"Allergies mean you are allergic to something. Something makes you sneeze or your eyes itch."

"I don't have allergies. Papa, Mom says that you have to stay away from strangers. Like when we are shopping, I'm supposed to stay close by her so nobody takes me away."

"Yes that is a smart thing to do."

"Can strangers come in and take me from my bed?"

"No, Granny Sienna and I are right here to protect you."

"Did you lock the doors?"

"Yes Carolina. All the doors are locked. You don't have to worry."

"Papa, I don't like the dark. Can you leave the light on? And can you tell me a story?"

"Why don't we turn the light off and I will tell you a story about the Quiet Light?"

"What's that Papa?"

"Watch the wall," Papa answered. "The Quiet Light is here to help you when you are afraid. It will keep watch over you all night, even when you are sleeping."

Suddenly, a light beam appeared on the upper part of the wall near the bedroom door. The light beam moved smoothly and swiftly across the wall to the corner of the adjacent wall of the room. It transferred seamlessly to the adjacent wall where it continued its path without losing any momentum. When it reached the end of the second wall it disappeared as mysteriously as it had appeared. The light beam had disappeared into nowhere. I didn't know whether to be scared or excited. To me, at five years old, it was like magic.

"Did you see it Carli? Did you see the Quiet Light?"

"Uh huh. Where did it go? Will it come back?"

"Just wait."

A few moments later the light beam appeared in exactly the same spot on the wall. It again moved swiftly and smoothly across the walls in exactly the same pattern.

"Carli, the Quiet Light will keep checking on you all night to make sure that you are safe, so you don't ever need to be afraid of the dark again."

After that night, when my Papa told me about the Quiet Light, I felt a new confidence and comfort. No longer was I worried about going to bed and being in the dark. I would just wait for the Quiet Light to appear and then I would close my eyes, reassured that I was being watched and guarded by this faithful entity.

From the time I was an infant, I spent a lot of time at my Wee Nanny and Papa's house. It was like a second home to me. My mother told me that I liked being there so much that my ideal was to live there. Of course, I wouldn't be able to live there unless my mom and dad, and my brother and sister came too. My Papa used to sing to us when we were babies and were being fussy. His favorite songs to sing were *Danny Boy* and *The Gambler*. He wasn't a very good singer but for some reason we found his voice soothing and would soon fall asleep in his arms. As a toddler I would follow my Papa around everywhere. He would play games with me. I would be Cinderella and he would be Prince Charming or Prince 'Carmin' as I called him. I would make up all the storylines and he had to play them out exactly as I told him. My mother likes to remind me still how I used to tell my Papa that he was my best friend in the whole world.

My Wee Nanny was called Wee Nanny because she just barely made it to five feet tall. She was actually less but would constantly argue that she wasn't.

My grandparents' house was in the country. Wee Nanny had designed it and had done all of the decorating. People who came to visit were always awestruck by her decorating talent. She loved antiques, which to me was just a bunch of old stuff. The one thing that I did like about Wee Nanny's house was her dollhouses. Wee Nanny had a hobby of building dollhouses and collecting miniatures. There were some that she would let me play with. I could amuse myself for hours playing with the tiny figurines, furniture, dishes, and other items of unique interest. There were other dollhouse items that I wasn't allowed to play with, I could "look but not touch." I did enjoy looking at them. I would stare at them wondering what it would be like to play with them.

My Papa wasn't concerned about how Wee Nanny decorated. He thought that she had a great talent and a good eye for making the house look nice. Quite often, Wee Nanny would move furniture around and when Papa got up in the middle of the night he would bang his knee or stub his toe on a piece of furniture that had just been moved that day. He was a very patient man.

Papa only had a few items that he treasured. One was an old rifle that hung above the fireplace. Papa told me that it was a 1700's Kentucky long rifle. To me it was just an old gun that didn't work and gathered dust from the fire, but it kind of looked neat.

Papa was always telling me stories, and there was always some sort of lesson he was trying to teach me with those stories. He would say to me, "Carli, you've got to be carefully taught."

Whenever Wee Nanny could tell that I had had enough of listening to him, she would raise her voice and bellow out, "Zachary Owens, leave the girl alone!"

Owens, that was my Papa's name, but apparently it wasn't his birth name. His birth name was William Alexander Dick. Papa changed his name to Zachary Owens when he was in his early twenties. He said that he didn't like having the last name Dick because of all the derogatory comments people used the name for, so he chose his own name. Papa always said that your name is important and should represent what you stand for and who you are.

When my mom and dad were naming me, my Papa wanted them to name me after some places that he had visited and was fond of in his younger days. He liked Virginia. He liked Savannah. He liked the Carolinas. Papa wanted to name me Savannah Virginia Carolina Owens. My mom and dad humored him a little and settled on Carolina. I am thankful that Papa didn't really take a big liking to Myrtle Beach or who knows what name I might have been called at school—Myrtle the Turtle?

During my elementary school days, I would go to my Granny and Papa's every day after school to do my homework. Upon stopping by one day, I went out to Papa's workshop to find him. Here he was preparing some boards for Wee Nanny and him to build another dollhouse. As I entered the workshop, he smiled and nodded.

My brother, sister, and I used to really like hanging out in Papa's workshop with him. He had some really neat things to fool around with. He would let us use his tools, even the power tools as long as we used them safely. He had interesting things hanging on the walls, including posters with inspirational sayings. If you asked him about any of them, he would go into a long story about what the meaning was and how we could apply it in our lives. This didn't mean much to me in public school. In high school though, I started to appreciate it more. Two of my favorites that he had posted on the wall were:

"The Price of Success is Hard Work" and *"We are Continually Faced with Great Opportunities, Brilliantly Disguised as Insoluble Problems."*

Sometimes, when Papa had us children as a captive audience, he would just start to recite poetry. One day he recited a poem by Robert Frost called "The Road Not Taken." At the time, I didn't understand why he liked it so much. But years later, after learning about his life, the reason became clear. It went:

> 'Two roads diverged in a yellow wood,
> And sorry I could not travel both
> And be one traveler, long I stood
> And looked down one as far as I could
> To where it bent in the undergrowth;
>
> Then took the other, as just as fair,
> And having perhaps the better claim,
> Because it was grassy and wanted wear;
> Though as for that the passing there
> Had worn them really about the same,
>
> And both that morning equally lay
> In leaves no step had trodden black.
> Oh! I kept the first for another day!
> Yet knowing how way leads on to way,
> I doubted if I should ever come back.
>
> I shall be telling this with a sigh

> Somewhere ages and ages hence:
> Two roads diverged in a wood, and I-
> I took the one less traveled by,
> And that has made all the difference.'

Of course it helped too that Papa had a fridge in his workshop that was always stocked with soda pop and ice cream treats which he let us help ourselves to while we were listening to his stories and reciting of poems.

When I arrived this particular day, Papa was running a board through the planer and motioned for me to grab the end of the board. I did so and then we did another and another. "How was school Carli?" Papa asked when he shut the planer off.

"Okay."

"Just okay?" he paused. I wasn't about to offer anything further. "What did you learn today?"

"Nuthin."

"Hmmm."

"Well okay—we're learning to write speeches. I hate it. I don't want to give a speech."

"Hmmm."

I could sense another story coming. With everything I did, every event in my life, every trial I faced, Papa always had a story. He always had some way of teaching me a life lesson. Sometimes they made a lot of sense and were valuable to me. Other times I just listened to him out of respect.

"Sometimes Carolina,"—he called me Carolina when a lecture was about to begin—"we have to do things we don't like to do or don't want to do to help us grow. Doing these things helps us to develop into better people."

I knew it, it was coming.

"Take for instance when I used to play hockey," he continued.

Wait a minute, I thought, my Papa used to play hockey? I just couldn't picture it. I couldn't even imagine it. He was only 5' 5", old, with grey hair and a pot belly. There were many things that my Papa told me he did that I wasn't quite sure whether they were true or not. Later, I would ask Wee Nanny. She confirmed it, he had in actual fact played hockey.

"When I played hockey," he continued. "I played left wing. Because of my size I was always hesitant going into the corners. Oh heck, I was scared, to put it plainly. I thought I was going to really get roughed up.

And a couple of times I did. The way I was playing wasn't helping our team. We missed a lot of scoring chances because I was afraid and let the opposing player beat me to the puck. Coach Armitage was getting really upset with me. After every game he would yell at me in the dressing room. He knew that I had the skating speed to get into the corner, get the puck and get out without getting creamed—if I could only overcome my fear."

"What happened Papa?" I asked out of respect. I didn't see how this had anything to do with me giving a speech nor did I care one iota about hockey.

"At the next practice, Coach Armitage lined the entire team up along the boards at about three feet away from the boards. He made me skate between the boards and the team. Every player on the team was to smash me into the boards. When I got to the end we had to do it all over again."

"Ouch! Did it help?"

"No. Next game I backed off again from going into the corners and coach Armitage yelled at me again. The next practice he did the same thing with the team smashing me against the boards again."

"I guess by then it worked?" I surmised.

"No. It still didn't work."

"So what did the coach do?"

"He put me on defense, where I was supposed to do the body checking. He said that I would stay there until I wasn't afraid to hit and be hit. One Sunday afternoon we were playing a team from Brampton that was overwhelmingly made up of large players. All of us were a little afraid. Every time any of our players went into corners they got creamed. We were really getting beat up badly. I had decided that I had enough and I was going to show that son-of—a . . . Armitage that I had enough of him too."

"One of the opposing players got a break away with just me back. He towered over me and probably weighed about eighty pounds more than I did. I decided that I was going to stop him. Just as he reached our blue line, I stepped into him. We both went down hitting the ice hard. My helmet went flying off my head and my glove and stick went flying in the air. The opposing player was shocked. He didn't know how much I was hurting—but I survived."

"In the dressing room, between the periods, Coach Armitage praised me saying that he had never seen such a great body check and that he hoped some of the bigger players on our team would show that kind of courage. Suddenly, I started to feel more confident. I had lost my fear of getting hit in the corners. Scoring goals started to come easier. The whole team was becoming more confident and enthusiastic. We went from losing every game to winning some."

"The following year, I became captain of the team and I was in the top ten scorers of the league. And this, Carolina, was all because Coach Armitage made me do something that I really didn't like doing. He made me face my fear. So you see Carolina, when you overcome your fear of giving speeches, you don't know what good benefits will come from it."

"Thanks Papa. I still don't want to give a speech."

"Did I ever tell you the story about climbing the ranger tower at Elliot Lake even though I was afraid of heights?"

"Yes Papa. You told me that when I didn't want to do gymnastics."

"How about when Henry Flecker took me up in his airplane?" . . .

When my Papa was fifteen years old, he had arranged for a summer job working with a contractor that did work for his father—my great grandfather. My great grandfather told the contractor not to hire my Papa. He told Papa that at fifteen he was too young to start working because he would be working for the rest of his life. Papa disagreed and left the house determined not to return until he had found a job for the summer. He walked all over town asking about any job openings. Of course the jobs were pretty much all taken by this time.

Henry Flecker used to own the local Texaco service station. It just so happened that Mr. Flecker was looking for a person to pump gas and clean up around the garage. Apparently he told my Papa that he was too small for the job, to which my Papa thanked him and with his head hung low started across the parking lot to the next business. Something moved Henry Flecker to open the office door and call out, "Oh, I guess you'll do. C'mon back." This was the start of a life-long friendship between the two. Papa worked very hard and kept the garage spic and span while ensuring that the customers were satisfied with their service. He worked six days per week, ten hours each day. Henry told people that Papa was the best employee that he ever hired. Mr. Flecker pushed Papa to go beyond his comfort zone and Papa often used these little stories to teach my brother, sister, and I lessons.

. . ."I think you told me that when I didn't want to go on the roller coaster with my little brother, Ryan."

"And I suppose that I told you about Henry Flecker sending me for coffee in his pick-up truck when I had never driven a standard shift before?"

"Yup Papa, heard that one too."

"What about . . ."

"Heard it too!"

"I see smarty. Well," he paused, "why don't you go in the house and see Granny Sienna? I think she was really looking forward to you coming today. Pretty sure she has something for you."

Inside, Wee Nanny or Granny Sienna as Papa called her was baking some cherry cheesecake tarts. This was her specialty and I loved them. "What were you and Papa talking about?" she asked.

"Oh, he was telling me some stuff about hockey."

"Oh your Papa and his stories."

Wee Nanny was very pretty and looked half her age. When I was just a toddler and she would take me places, people would think that she was too young to be a mother. People were then shocked to find out that she was actually my grandmother. She was always busy working in her gardens, which is what I think kept her so healthy and young looking. She loved planting and growing everything. Papa, on the other hand hated gardening.

That brings me to As Far As. As Far As was a friend of Papa's. He actually lived with Papa and Granny Sienna. That wasn't his real name of course but that's what Papa called him. Papa gave him that nickname years ago because he started almost every sentence by saying *'As far as . . .'* If he didn't start this way then he would stutter terribly. He was born with some mental disabilities that prevented him from learning to read or write. Papa would sometimes take him for lunch and I would tag along. Papa was very patient showing As Far As pictures on the menu to help him find out what he wanted to eat. I later realized that this showed great kindness and patience on my Papa's part. As Far As loved doing gardening and yard work so he would help Granny Sienna with this work instead of Papa. Papa was quite happy with this arrangement.

Half way through my first year of high school I finally got my wish to live at my Wee Nanny and Papa's house. My Mom told me that it was so that I could attend a better high school that was closer to where my grandparents lived. But I knew that it was because my Dad and I just kept butting heads. My Dad thought that I was being trouble. Wee Nanny on the other hand said that I was just a little bit head strong and that I was just like my Dad. She raised him so I guess she would know.

Sitting by the fireplace one winter evening, I started to rag on my Dad. My Papa said that my Dad only disciplines me because he loves me and cares about how I turn out. I told Wee Nanny and Papa that he was always criticizing me and how he was always accusing me of things that I wasn't guilty of before he knew all of the facts. "Do you remember the last time that you accused someone of something that they weren't guilty of?" Papa asked.

"No."

"Think really hard."

"I can't think of anything," I offered.

"How about last week," Wee Nanny broke in, "when you thought that your friend Megan was talking about you behind your back. You were mad at her. It turned out that she wasn't talking about you at all."

"You're right Nanny."

"Now," Papa continued, "can you remember the first time that someone accused you of something that you weren't guilty of?"

"That's easy. In grade one the janitor sent me to the office for throwing stones at the school window. All I was doing was standing there watching some older boys throw the stones. When the principal finally let me go to my classroom, my teacher told the whole class that I had been a bad girl."

"Isn't it interesting that most of us, like you, can't remember the last time that we accused someone wrongfully but we can remember way back to the first time we were accused wrongfully?"

"So what are you saying Papa?"

"Maybe you should try to look at things from your Dad's standpoint."

"I don't get it Papa."

"Take a look at this baby block," Papa said as he reached into a nearby toy box. "What do you see?"

"I see the letter 'E'"

"Hmm, I see the letter 'V', but then I am looking at a different side of the same block. You see we all view things from our own perspective. Take for example when you were a kid and you would see a fire truck whirring by. How would that make you feel?"

"It was kind of exciting to see, Papa."

"True, to you it was exciting. But to the people who lived in the house it was heading to it was frightening, maybe even devastating."

"Okay, I think I get it now."

When spring arrived we would sit out on the front porch if the evenings were warm enough. Wee Nanny and Papa had a modest house but it did have a nice view of the Grand River from the front porch. They would love to sit on the porch and just take in the view. Across the road, down near the river was Myles Stafford's homestead. Myles was a very wealthy farmer. He owned thousands of acres in the area as well as cattle and chicken operations. Because of his wealth, he could afford to make his property so picturesque that it could put to shame any picture on a calendar. An artist could not recreate such a beautiful setting as Myles Stafford had created. Papa used to tell Wee Nanny and me that we should be thankful that Myles Stafford was so rich because looking from our front porch over at his acreage we had one of the nicest views in the county. And Papa would add, we didn't have to pay a nickel for it or work to maintain it, Myles Stafford did all of that for us.

"Well, I wouldn't mind having just a little bit of his money," I told Papa one evening.

"Carli, some people say that money isn't everything. Then they add it is the only thing. Others say that money means nothing."

"What do you think Papa?" I couldn't believe that I was actually having such an adult conversation with my Papa. I remembered as a little girl it was always Papa counseling me, telling me stories, and coaching me. Now I was actually asking him for his thoughts on a matter.

"Can I show you something from the Bible?"

Papa wasn't a Bible thumper or a fanatic as some were but he did read the Bible often and he would quote a scripture to me or show me a scripture in the Bible now and then. Usually if he was sitting on the front porch having his tea, he would have his Bible next to him so that he could read a little bit of it.

Opening his Bible, he began, "It's in first Timothy, chapter six, versus nine and ten. It reads:

'Those who are determined to be rich fall into temptation and a snare and many senseless and hurtful desires which plunge men into destruction and ruin. For the love of money is a root of all sorts of injurious things and by reaching out for this love some have been led astray from the faith and have stabbed themselves all over with many pains.'

"So what does that mean Papa?"

"Many people have sacrificed their family life, their friendships and even their relationship with God to pursue money because they love it. There is nothing wrong with having money. It is more how you perceive money—what's in your heart."

"Well, I like money Papa. I can buy clothes, go out with my friends, and you know, just buy stuff."

"As I said Carli, there is nothing wrong with having money. It is how we view it, how we think about it. Do you suppose that if Myles Stafford is sitting over on his front porch having a cup of tea that his tea tastes any better than mine?"

"Most likely not."

"How about the sunset out there to the east, do you think it is any more beautiful for Myles Stafford?"

"Definitely not. You are both looking at the same sky."

"Money can sure be a help in this life," Papa began his counsel. "It can buy you things and take you places that you can't have or go to without money. But in the end, when we pass away, we can't take any of it with us."

"I know that Papa," I snickered.

"When we are gone what we have left behind are the memories that people such as our friends and relatives, our associates, our neighbors, have of us. What is left is our good name or bad, the name that we have made with our creator. So if we have money in this life then it is best to use it for the good and do what we can to help others. If we don't have money then we should be content with sustenance and covering and still do good toward others with what we do have."

"But Papa wouldn't you rather be rich?"

"I had that opportunity once Carli. I had that opportunity once."

I didn't ask and Papa didn't tell. I could sense that I was touching on some memory that he just wanted to leave buried for now.

Growing up, I had a best friend named Alyssa. We did practically everything together. So at the beginning of grade eleven when she told me she was planning to move to Edmonton when we were done school and attend university there, I was devastated. As soon as I heard the news I headed straight to my grandparents' house.

"What's on your mind today Sunshine?" Papa asked. He could always tell right away when I was upset.

"Alyssa and I were supposed to go to university together at McMaster in Hamilton. We were both going to take Phys. Ed. and then become Phys Ed. teachers. We planned to share an apartment in Hamilton. Now Alyssa wants to move out to Edmonton to live with her sister and go to school there."

"I see."

"She said that her sister is okay if I come too. But I don't want to leave Keegan. Papa what am I going to do? Alyssa has been my best friend since public school but I love Keegan. I can't bear the thought of being away from either one of them."

"Ah, the best laid plans of mice and men," Papa remarked.

"What do you mean Papa?"

"Robbie Burns, an old Scottish poet, once wrote about a mouse whose nest he had disturbed when plowing a field. It was a lesson for us that no matter how much we plan for the future, we really don't know what is around the corner for us. Do you remember last summer when we had a campfire out back and we found that a mouse had built a nest in the fire pit?"

"I do. We didn't see the nest until after we started the fire."

"That's right," Papa concurred. "That mother mouse didn't know that we were going to have a campfire there. She thought that she had planned well and found a perfect spot to raise her young safely. We moved the babies so that they would be safe."

"But I remember she kept taking them back towards the fire."

"That's right Carolina. She didn't know what we knew. She couldn't see the big picture, so to speak. She didn't know that we were actually trying to save her and her family."

"So, Papa, what does that have to do with my problem?"

"Well maybe it would be better for you to go to school in Edmonton. Maybe there are opportunities there that you just can't see."

"But Papa, what if it's the wrong decision?"

"How could it be the wrong decision?"

"What if my life turns into an entire mess?"

"Then you readjust. You learn what you can from it and move on. What's behind you becomes history. It`s the past and you can't change it. You can only change your future. Didn't that mother mouse finally see that we were moving her babies away from the fire?"

"Yeah."

"Then she changed her plan. She stopped trying to take them back to the nest."

I always referred to this as Papa's mouse story. He told me that an author named John Steinbeck wrote a novel called "Of Mice and Men" and that I should read it to broaden my cultural knowledge. I told him that I'd wait for the movie to come out. Papa said there already was a movie and a good one at that. I didn't fully understand the mouse story until one day Papa's neighbor, Mr. Perkins, came over to see Papa when he was doing some more woodwork for Wee Nanny. I happened to be out in the workshop with my Papa when Mr. Perkins came by.

Mr. Perkins seemed to me to be a bit of a flake—kind of scatterbrained. Papa explained that Mr. Perkins wasn't always that way. He said that he and Mr. Perkins used to have some really good chats about life and world events. In fact, several years earlier Mr. Perkins had told Papa about his and his wife's plans to retire and travel within five years. Their finances were going to be in good shape and they were both in great health, it was the perfect time. But then their daughter and son-in-law were in a car accident that left their daughter with brain damage. She had to learn to walk, talk, and everything all over again. Her husband found the whole situation too stressful and ended up divorcing her, so Mr. and Mrs. Perkins took her back in. It was terribly hard on them.

Papa continued to explain to me that then Mr. and Mrs. Perkins' married son went through a divorce and he moved back home with them also. Their plans to travel were temporarily, if not indefinitely, on hold. A few years went by, and then one evening when Mr. and Mrs. Perkins were on their way home from the theatre in Orangeville, Mr. Perkins swerved their car to miss a deer sending their car into oncoming traffic. Mrs. Perkins was killed. My goodness, I thought, could this man suffer any more?

I was finally starting to understand the mouse story and why whenever things went wrong my Papa would say, "Ah, the best laid plans of mice and men."

Back to my situation with Alyssa.

"But Papa, what about Keegan?"

"Well Sunshine, that's a matter of the heart and matters of the heart are your Granny Sienna's specialty. Why don't you go and get her advice."

As I walked toward the house, Papa called out,

"Never fear the future Carolina."

Inside the house, Wee Nanny was cooking dinner. "Nanny, should I stay here and be with Keegan or should I move out west and go to school with Alyssa?"

"Could you set the table for me Carli?"

I was sure that Wee Nanny heard me.

"What should I do," I prompted as I got out the plates and silverware to show that I was co-operating with her.

"Well, why would you stay here with Keegan?"

"Because I love him."

"Are you sure it is true love?"

"Oh yes! Absolutely." I commenced putting the plates and silverware on the table, "Well how do I know? Papa said that you were an expert at affairs of the heart."

"He did, did he? Why do you love Keegan?"

"He's so handsome Nanny. All the girls are jealous of me."

"Is there anything else?"

"I feel so good when I am around him and he makes me laugh."

"True love Carli," Wee Nanny counseled, "is based on more than just good looks. Don't let your heart misguide you. True love is based on caring unselfishly about the other person, putting their interests ahead of your own."

"Oh, I do Nanny."

"How about Keegan? Does he put your interests ahead of his?"

"Sometimes—but not always."

"It sounds like you need some more time to get to know each other better before you can call it true love. Get to know Keegan's personality better and his spiritual qualities. You have to be attracted to the total person."

"Was that how it was with you and Papa?"

"Papa was so handsome. All the girls were jealous of me."

We both burst out laughing. Nanny continued to explain the difference between true love and infatuation. We also talked about friendship and Wee Nanny explained that there are friends of the heart and friends of the road and that Alyssa will always be a friend of the heart.

As Wee Nanny and I were chatting, I noticed a car pull in the laneway. An older black man got out at the end of the laneway and made his way to the front door. He walked very slowly and with a limp.

"Hello," he said politely when I opened the door. "I was wondering if Zachary Owens lives here?"

"He does," I replied. "He's my Papa."

"Well I'll be," he smiled. His smile unveiled several teeth missing yet it was a warm and endearing smile. Perhaps it was his eyes. His smile seemed to be coming straight from his heart. "I's your, I's your . . ." he hesitated as Papa came around the corner of the house and approached the front porch.

When their eyes caught sight of each other both men smiled a contented smile as though they were each meeting a long lost brother or something.

"I's your Papa's friend," the man continued. He was quite a bit older than Papa.

When Wee Nanny caught sight of the man, she came running out of the house and threw her arms around him. The three of them sat down on the porch and talked. I was sent in the house to make tea for them all. But since one of the front windows was open a bit, I tried to listen in on the conversation.

"I found it Zach, all of it," I overheard the old man say. Who was this guy I wondered and what did he find? "Then I re-hid all of it—well most of it. I had to cash in some to keep myself going all of these years."

"Where did you hide it Fripp?" Papa asked.

"I hid it all over the United States and Canada. I even took some of it back to Europe. I documented everything, in code of course, and all the documents are in this bag." Papa's friend had been carrying an old, beat up brown case with him. It apparently was an old Civil War saddle bag. He had pulled out some papers to show Papa while they were talking. "I want you to have this Zach. A lot of it should be yours anyway."

"Thanks Fripp. I'm getting too old to chase after treasure."

"There's something that you need to know Zach. It's about Jacques Falstaff."

"You mean B.S. Jack?"

"Yes, he . . ." The tea kettle started to whistle and I couldn't hear what Mr. Fripp was saying.

When Mr. Fripp went away, he left the saddle bag with Papa. When Papa came in the house, he hung the saddle bag just inside the door on a hook with some of his Civil War memorabilia. I happened to be standing right there.

"When I die," he instructed, "you are to take this bag and go through the papers inside. Do you understand?"

"Yes, but what's in there?"

"Never mind for now, just make sure that you do as I say."

"Okay Papa."

He seemed to be more serious about this than I had ever seen him.

Senior year came and went and with it went Alyssa. In the end I chose love, or at least that's what I told myself as to why I wasn't going, but in reality I was making the safer choice. I knew my Papa and Granny Sienna were disappointed and felt like I was missing out on an amazing experience, but for the first time in my whole life Papa didn't lecture me, or counsel me, or tell me another one of his life-lesson-filled stories. Maybe he realized I had reached an age where my choices were finally my own, but so were the consequences. Later, on his death bed, he would tell me the real reason. He told me that I had to build my own wealth of stories to tell my grandchildren when I got older, and choosing "infatuation" over adventure because it was "safe" would be a good one.

Two weeks into my first year at McMaster, Keegan and I broke up—so much for true love, and basing my entire life course on it. I went home for the weekend to visit and break the news to my Papa and Wee Nanny. Papa just nodded when I told him the news, but he seemed pleased, though he did give me a consoling pat on the head. Like he said before, he wasn't good with matters of the heart.

While we sat having tea on the front porch that night, Papa was unusually quiet. But then, after much forethought it seemed, he said,

"There are plenty of fish in the sea Carolina. Did I ever tell you that I was in love with another girl before I met your Granny Sienna?"

All the multitude of stories Papa had told me throughout my childhood and young adult life, and yet he had never told me that one. I was intrigued.

"You never told me that Papa!"

Papa took a sip of his tea then placed it beside him looking out over the front yard as he gathered his memories. I settled into my chair, with the feeling that this was going to be a great story.

"Well," Papa commenced, "her name was Erica. It all started in Charleston, South Carolina. Charleston," he continued, "is one of the most beautiful places on earth. It wasn't far from there in a place called Beaufort where I met and fell in love with Granny Sienna."

CHARLESTON, SOUTH CAROLINA

MAY 1976

William Dick found himself standing on the corner of Queen and Meeting Street in downtown Charleston, South Carolina. It was the beginning of May of 1976. He had just eaten lunch at Poogan's Porch with his long-time girlfriend Erica. They had been together since grade eleven in high school. The sun was beating down on the concrete and asphalt around him radiating a heat upward that normally he could drink in and enjoy. Growing up in Canada, he had spent most summers working as a laborer and was used to being out in the hot sun, but this Charleston sun was a whole new level of heat. He hadn't been in South Carolina very long when he realized that he was going to need a haircut and a good shave. His friends back home nicknamed him Serpico, after Al Pacino, because of his full beard. In fact, it was Erica who encouraged him to grow it; she told him she liked the way he looked with it. But now he stood there, suitcase in hand as Erica drove away. Was he doing the right thing? Should he have fought more for her to stay? He wondered. They had planned to spend the summer driving through the eastern United States, looking at historical sites. This was Erica's idea since she was studying history at the University of Western Ontario in London. Two days into the trip, as they reached Charleston, Erica said that she wanted to see other people and that she had been already seeing other guys when she was away at school. Bill was crushed and heartbroken, he begged her to reconsider, but her mind seemed to be made up. She just didn`t love him like she used to, she said. Having lunch at Poogan's Porch was pre-planned. Erica said that a school-mate had told her about it and recommended that she try it out while in Charleston. It was there at lunch that she broke the devastating news to Bill.

Bill, being the nice guy that he was, let Erica take most of the money that they brought for the trip. He still loved her and was concerned about her having enough money to make it back to Canada. But now he felt like a sucker. Erica owned the car, so not only was he broke, he was stranded too. There he stood, suitcase in hand, watching the only person he knew between Toronto and Charleston, drive away.

Being lunch time, minute by minute hundreds of people were walking around and past Bill. They had no idea of how alone and sick he felt as he watched the person who had been his best friend, his lover, disappear from his life. The Charleston heat was making his hand sweaty. With drooping shoulders, he let his suitcase fall to the sidewalk. He didn't even feel like picking it up.

"Did you get rolled mate?" a voice came from near the entrance to Poogan's Porch behind Bill. There was no response. "Did you get rolled mate?" the tall Australian called out again.

"I'm sorry. Were you talking to me?" Bill responded.

"I don't see anybody else who looks like he just lost everything."

"It's a long story."

"What's your name mate?" the stranger asked in a friendly tone as he approached.

"William. William Dick. Friends just call me Bill."

"Well, just Bill, maybe you didn't get rolled but you look pretty lost. You have a suitcase. You must need a place to stay."

"I do," Bill said gloomily.

"A friend of mine owns the Alvermay Inn. Most of the people that stay there are either prostitutes or winos or they got rolled—you know mugged. The place ain't pretty but it is cheap. I stay there myself when I'm in Charleston. You interested?"

"Sure. Why not?" This was the first bit of good news Bill had had all day.

"Where you from mate?"

"Toronto. Well actually Grand Valley, about an hour and a half from Toronto. I really appreciate this . . . uh . . . I didn`t get your name?" Bill asked the stranger.

"Jacques Pierre Falstaff. My mother was French Canadian hence the Jacques Pierre. My acquaintances call me Jack. My friends call me BS Jack."

"BS?"

"Yeah. Short for Bull Scat Jack."

"I'm afraid to ask," Bill commented as the two men walked east along Queen Street. "Do they call you Bull Scat Jack because you're full of bull?" Bill tried to make a joke and snickered to himself but he was still feeling downhearted.

"I prefer to call it useless information," Jack answered. "What brings you to Charleston?" Jack asked.

"Just a place I`ve never been. I planned on doing some sightseeing and studying some history. It looks like those plans have changed though." With head hung low, Bill whispered to himself, "Ah, the best laid plans of mice and men."

"I thought maybe with a name like Dick you were researching some family history. That name has quite a historical significance in this area, although not common knowledge." Jack continued.

"How so?" Bill enquired.

"There's a story that Alexander Dick financed the American Revolution," Jack said.

"My middle name is Alexander."

"William Alexander Dick. That's really interesting mate. Don't suppose you're Scottish too?"

"My grandfather was from Scotland," Bill replied.

As Bill Dick and Jack Falstaff walked east along Queen Street, Bill was half listening to Jack and half thinking about his newfound singleness. He hoped Erica would be okay on her own getting back to the Valley. What kind of a person worries about the girl who just ripped their heart out? He thought. Rounding the corner onto East Bay Street, the Old Exchange and Provost Dungeon came into view.

"Well there is the Alvermay," Jack pointed out as the two men reached Broad Street, capturing Bill`s attention once again.

The Alvermay, located at 120 East Bay Street, was one of the oldest buildings in Charleston that was still being used as a pub and hotel. It actually was the oldest continuous liquor establishment in the United States. It sat directly to the south of the Old Exchange and Provost Dungeon on the south-east corner of East Bay and Exchange Street. The Alvermay was very plain looking from the outside. It didn't have the remarkable, ornate architectural characteristics that the surrounding buildings and almost all of Charleston seemed to have. Yet, beyond its faded stucco exterior, the tiny building housed a bar and some hotel rooms. The two-storey building had an entrance that faced directly toward the intersection of the streets with a window on each side of the door and a series of windows running south along the building. There was an extension on the back of the structure that housed a kitchen. The kitchen then backed onto an alley which entered onto Exchange Street.

Bill and Jack entered the Inn. It was very dimly lit and smelled of spilled beer that had been left on carpets. Adding to that was a musty smell from patrons coming in with wet footwear when it had been raining. To the left of the entry was a hall that led toward washrooms and a staircase to the second floor. Straight ahead and to the left, just beyond the hallway, was the bar. In front of the bar were about ten sets of wooden tables and chairs with seating for four at each. The tables had glossy finishes with words and etchings carved into them by past patrons. Off to the far right, in the corner was a man sitting with a woman who Bill thought must have been one of the prostitutes that Jack spoke about. Just inside the door to the right, was another man who had passed out with his head down on the table. He still had a half-full mug of draught beer sitting in front of him. With one hand still on his mug of beer, the man was drooling onto the table. Jack walked over and stuck the man's hand in his beer and the man urinated in his pants. Jack laughed and Bill thought that this was just plain mean.

At the very end of the room, two men were playing darts. They were being watched by a third man who obviously wasn't part of their group but continually provided his input on the quality of their dart throwing. The two dart throwers just ignored him.

The walls of the Alvermay were covered with dark mahogany which added to the overall darkness of the room. The wood itself was very rich looking and told of better more prosperous days of past. Pictures of the Civil War and the American Revolution dotted the walls.

Three tiffany chandeliers hung over the bar further indicating that at one time this was a thriving gathering place. The chandeliers now, however, were dusty and you could see cobwebs on the tops of them. This is a dive, Bill thought to himself.

From beyond the bar, Bill could hear a radio playing. *". . . You can check out any time you like, but you can never leave, Welcome to the Hotel California . . ."* Bill recognized the newly released Eagles song and hoped that this wasn't some sort of forewarning. He set his suitcase down and wiped the sweat from his forehead with the back of his hand.

"Fripp!" Jack called out. "Fripp, I've brought you a guest."

A middle aged, black man hobbled out from the kitchen that was located behind the bar. He was wearing a white apron and drying his hands with a towel. Fripp had a bald head and grey stubble beard. "Humph! I suppose you want a freebee," he said, giving Bill the once over.

"No. No, I have money. Not much—but some," Bill said.

"Okay man. Thirty five dollars for the week. If you need a job, you can do dishes for me. I'll pay you two dollars for one hour."

"Sure," Bill answered. "I'll take the room and the job."

"Hah! Wait till you see the room," Jack joked.

"Here's a key for room number four upstairs. It's across from Jack's room, number three. You can start work tomorrow night. Stow your gear upstairs then come on back down," Fripp instructed. "What's your name son?"

"William Dick. Bill."

As Bill was walking up the stairs to his room, he overheard Fripp ask Jack, "So what's the story on this one Jack?"

"I don't really know Fripp. He just looked like he needed a friend."

Upstairs, Bill opened the door to room number four. It was quite small. There was a single cot, a dresser with a mirror above it and a fan. He looked around—no washroom? At least it didn't smell as bad as the bar area downstairs, he thought. As Bill threw his suitcase on the cot, a mouse ran out from underneath. The wallpaper was peeling off the walls. The only window in the room opened onto East Bay Street. Bill struggled but got it open to let some air in. The window ledge itself was coated with several months' worth of dust, dead flies and beetles.

Back downstairs Bill went to sit at a table near the window. "No. No, not there!" Fripp yelled from behind the bar. "That's the mad Scotsman's chair."

Bill jerked back almost tripping, "The who? The what?"

Jack started to laugh, "Fripp thinks there is a ghost of a mad Scotsman living here. No one is allowed to sit in that chair. That's his chair. If anyone sits in that chair then he trashes the place at night. Fripp has to leave a shot of Scotch on the table for the fellow. If Fripp doesn't then the ghost trashes the place at night."

"Fripp," Bill started, "there are no such things as ghosts."

"That's what I tell him," Jack agreed.

"How do you know Bill? You haven't seen the big guy!"

"It's in the Bible," Bill responded. "There are no ghosts. There are fallen angels which the Bible refers to as demons—but no ghosts."

"Well whatever it is Bill, he likes his Scotch."

Bill and Jack sat down at a table near where the two men had been playing darts. "Your ancestors were Scottish then mate? Buy me a beer and I'll tell you a story."

From behind the bar, Fripp overheard the conversation and called out, "Don't listen to Bull Scat Jack, buddy. He'll just fill your head with false stories and con you into buying him beers. He just likes to hear himself talk."

"I haven't got any money to buy him a beer anyway. I have to keep it to pay for the room," Bill chuckled.

"Uh huh," Jack acknowledged. "You see Fripp. He can't buy me a beer anyway."

"So Jack, you still going to tell him a story?" Fripp challenged.

"Ahhh why not? Sit down here mate. Fripp set us up with a couple of beers. This young fella here has got to know about his family's history," Jack said.

Fripp brought two beers over and set them on the table. "Don't believe everything Jack tells ya son. They don't call him Bull Scat Jack for nuthin'."

Jean-Claude Dupuis or Fripp as he was commonly known was the offspring of a mother who was part Seminole Indian and a black Frenchman from Louisiana. He was raised by his aunt on Fripp Island hence the nickname Fripp. When he was a teenager, Fripp was bitten by an alligator and lost a piece of his left calf muscle, so his left leg didn't fully straighten out causing him to walk with a limp.

Bill thought that there was something familiar about Jack but he just couldn't put his finger on it. Jack was very tall and handsome in appearance. His muscular build gave the notion that he was an athlete of some sort. He spoke with confidence and charm. But he was almost too charming to the point where Bill wondered if it was put on. He had met guys like Jack before and they were almost always not to be trusted. Nevertheless, Bill was where he was at. His situation was what it was. He had a room for at least a couple of nights and a job to earn some money for food. If Bill had to humor Jack by listening to his story then so be it. Besides, Bill didn't have anywhere else to go at this point.

"So there was a meeting between George Washington, Thomas Jefferson, and Benjamin Franklin," Jack began.

"This should be good," Fripp mumbled sarcastically from behind the bar.

"Are you are trying to tell me that my ancestry had something to do with Washington, Jefferson, and Franklin? Did you forget that I'm a Canadian, eh?"

"Do you want to hear the story or don't you?"

"Well, sure I do, but if it's going to be that far-fetched then I think you need to buy me another beer," Bill was just swallowing the last of the first beer that Fripp had brought him. "This American beer is just like water compared to what we drink in Canada."

"Fripp, bring the *Canadian* here another beer."

"Didn't you say you spent some time in Canada, Jack?" Fripp asked as he set two more beers on the table. "Some university or something wasn't it?"

"Yeah, yeah. Now let me get on with this story," Jack protested.

Bill thought for a minute that Erica had said she had a teaching assistant for one of her classes who was Australian. She never mentioned his name, but no—there couldn't be any connection.

As I was saying, there was a meeting between George Washington, Thomas Jefferson, and Benjamin Franklin."

"Shouldn't you start with 'Once upon a time'?" Fripp joked.

"Alright," Jack commanded, "that's enough." Jack paused and then started again, "Their meeting took place in Williamsburg, Virginia at the Raleigh Tavern. The year was 1771."

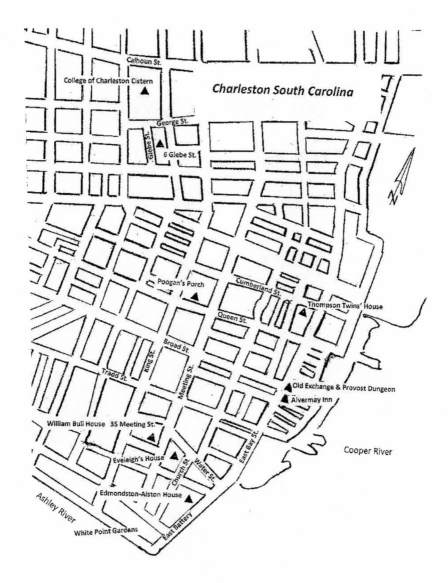

Charleston, South Carolina

At the Raleigh Tavern

Williamsburg, 1771

As darkness was falling in Williamsburg, the light from the lanterns reflected in the faces of the two men sitting in the small, private room adjacent to the main room inside the Raleigh Tavern. This was one of several small rooms where groups of men would often gather to play cards and drink or enjoy a meal. Of course there was a main dining area as well. Here groups of men could enjoy their meals while talking about the latest news from England and other parts of the colonies. When the governor dissolved the House of Burgesses, the leaders of Virginia gathered here at the Raleigh to plan their strategy against the King of England. Upstairs, there were several rooms where patrons could spend the night or rent a room for an extended stay. The exterior of the Raleigh was painted white with green shutters. There were seven dormers across the front roof line. A small canopy-type roof protected the front entrance.

The two men sat in silence, waiting patiently. There was a growing tension in Virginia, as there was in the entire colony. This was a nervous tension that there was an impending event about to take place that would shatter life as the colonists knew it. There was a feeling among the colonists that their existence was fragile and at any moment could break. Through the walls could be heard the sound of billiard balls striking each other as men played billiards on a table in the main room. Muffled conversation by patrons in the main room created a soft background droning noise.

The shorter, balding man was writing on parchment with his quill. His name was Benjamin Franklin. The other man, Thomas Jefferson, was pacing anxiously and then sat down at the table. Ben Franklin raised his head as the sound of horse hooves neared the tavern. With the curtains open, outside in the moonlight, he could see the rider dismount and approach the Raleigh entrance.

As the rider entered the tavern the billiard players stopped and raised their eyes. They knew this man and respected him. Henry Wetherburn, the tavern owner stood behind the bar cleaning some glasses. Looking straight at the rider but not saying anything, he nodded his head toward the door of the room where the two men were waiting. From inside the room, the two men could hear the rider's footsteps approach as the floors creaked under his impressive stature.

The door swung open and the taller, slenderer of the two men who were waiting, stood up. With outstretched hand, "George," he welcomed him.

"Thomas. Benjamin." The rider responded with a nod to each as he removed his hat and cape.

"How was your journey?" Ben Franklin asked while rolling up his document and setting his inkwell aside.

"Fine, but I am thirsty. How about a glass of that flip there?"

George Washington pulled a chair up to the table and he and Thomas Jefferson sat down joining Ben Franklin.

"Allow me," Franklin offered filling a glass from the pitcher and sliding it toward Washington.

In the corner there was a small fire burning. Washington took a drink from his glass and asked, "What does the situation look like?"

"It seems we have exhausted all attempts for a peaceful resolution. I am afraid that we are going to have to resort to revolution of a physical nature," Franklin answered.

"I on the other hand," Jefferson cut in, "don't agree. I think we still need to pursue peaceful methods."

"The British don't understand peaceful methods Thomas!" Franklin snapped.

"Benjamin," Jefferson continued. "I am afraid that we are going down a road that will end in death if we don't succeed. Not just my death and your death, but that of our children and many innocent colonists. I am not afraid of war with Britain. I just think we need to continue our attempts to come to a peaceful resolution."

Washington rose and moved toward the fire. He rubbed his hands together and held them in front of the fire to warm them from his ride in the cold evening air. "There's no other way Ben?" he queried.

"Not as far as I am concerned."

"And Thomas?"

"There still is hope."

"Hope," Washington pondered. "It would be good if the five colonists who were killed last year at the Boston Massacre had hope. Theirs is gone and I am sure that ours will be too if we do not prepare ourselves for the eventuality that we will have to war with Britain to gain our independence."

"George," Jefferson implored. "I don't think that I need to remind you that not all colonists are in agreement with us. There are those who wish to remain loyal to the Crown."

"I realize that Thomas. But why should the people in the colony go bankrupt and starve in order to pay the 130,000,000 pounds sterling debt that King George and Queen Charlotte have racked up?"

"George," Jefferson reminded, "many of our colonists are enjoying prosperity because the Royal Treasury spent the money on the French and Indian War. Now the Crown must maintain troops in Nova Scotia and other parts of Canada in order to protect theirs and our interests."

"Yes Thomas," Washington conceded. "However, the Crown's immense taxation policies are crushing us."

"We will need arms and supplies in order to fight the British. The colonists do not have the resources to equip and support an army."

"I know a man," Franklin jumped in. "I know a man who can finance an entire army."

"Who is he?" Washington asked.

"He is Alexander Dick. Dr. Alexander Dick. Sir Alexander Dick."

"Never heard of him," Washington responded.

"Sir Alexander Dick was the president of the College of Physicians in Edinburgh."

"There you have it George!" Jefferson piped up. "Franklin is stuck on this legend that the Templar's Treasure is in Scotland. Are you going to go get the treasure so that we can fight a war?"

"Thomas, whether you or I, or any of our Masonic brothers believe or don't believe in the Templar's Treasure has nothing to do with getting funding for the war with Britain. I tell you Alexander Dick has the resources to help us."

"Why would he help us? Is he one of our Masonic brothers?" Washington asked.

"No," Franklin answered. "Unfortunately he is not. Dick has been invited to join our brotherhood but refuses to do so."

"Then why are you so sure that he will help us?" Jefferson enquired.

"He is a good friend of mine. I know what drives him."

"And what might that be?" Washington prompted.

"Revenge."

"Revenge is not a good motivator Ben. It usually spells disaster for the one seeking vengeance. The bible says, 'Vengeance is mine says Yahweh.'" Jefferson continued, "Maybe we had better stay away from this man and his money."

"What do you suggest Thomas?" asked Washington. "Do you know of other people to get the funding from?"

"Not right at this moment."

"That's the problem. We are running out of moments," continued Washington. "Let's have Benjamin try to get funding from this Alexander Dick fellow. At the same time, Thomas, you see what you can do using peaceful methods. Our next problem is what happens if we actually get the money from Dick? Every entry port into the colonies is guarded by the British. Every shipment is checked. Do you not think the British are going to become alarmed when they see shipments of arms, supplies, and money coming here from Scotland?"

"I have thought about that. I will take Dr. Will Pasteur and Dr. John Galt with me to Edinburgh. We will travel under the pretense of my introducing these two men to Dr. Dick, in order for them to further their studies in medicine. When Alexander Dick ships supplies to us, they will come buried in shipments of medical supplies and be delivered to Dr. Pasteur's or Dr. Galt's apothecary shops."

"Is there anything we can do for Dr. Dick?" Washington asked.

"Beat the British!" Franklin mused. "Dick enjoys hunting. The last time we met, he asked me to get him one of those new Kentucky Long Rifles."

"That's the least we could do. There is one outside with my saddle. I will give it to you before I leave. When will you depart for Scotland Benjamin?"

"I will go to see Pasteur and Galt tonight and then we will leave on the next ship sailing from Yorktown."

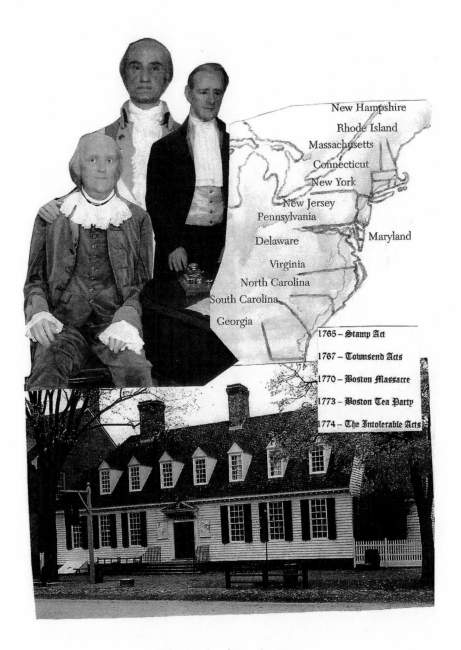

New Hampshire
Rhode Island
Massachusetts
Connecticut
New York
New Jersey
Pennsylvania
Delaware
Maryland
Virginia
North Carolina
South Carolina
Georgia

1765 – Stamp Act
1767 – Townsend Acts
1770 – Boston Massacre
1773 – Boston Tea Party
1774 – The Intolerable Acts

The Seeds of Revolution

Pasteur and Galt were both very intelligent men. Dr. Pasteur had opened an apothecary shop in Williamsburg in 1759. Dr. Galt had opened his apothecary shop in 1768. Both men had felt the effects of The Stamp Act passed by Britain in 1765 and The Townsend Act passed by Britain in 1767. They looked forward to freedom from harsh and unfair rule by Britain. They gladly responded to Ben Franklin's invite to be part of the covert operation to get arms, supplies, and funds for the colonies. Galt also looked forward to the opportunity to meet with fellow physicians in Edinburgh and especially Dr. Alexander Dick. Pasteur on the other hand was looking for adventure. Each was about to get what they wanted.

As they pulled away from shore at Yorktown, Pasteur and Galt were standing on the ship's deck, waving good-bye to their families. Pasteur turned to Galt, "Do you really think that Dr. Dick knows where the Templar's Treasure is?"

"Look, Will. Don't believe every story that Ben Franklin tells you. He could talk a black bear into giving up his fur coat. If there is a treasure, I'm sure Ben will find it."

The route would take them across the Atlantic Ocean, north past Ireland toward the Shetland Islands, and then south along the east coast of Scotland to Edinburgh.

PRESTONFIELD HOUSE

SCOTLAND

1771

Lined by a canopy of trees that stood like witnesses at a church wedding, the laneway to Prestonfield House beckoned them toward their dreams as Ben Franklin, John Galt, and Will Pasteur approached the impressive structure. The pillars on each side of the doorway framed an entry into a new world, a new hope for each man. Benjamin Franklin saw it as an entrance to the opportunity and hope for a Democratic Republic in the colony—free from tyrannical British rule. John Galt saw the entrance as an opportunity to meet and learn from the renowned Dr. Alexander Dick and other physicians so that he could bring that knowledge and experience back to America. Will Pasteur viewed the entrance as an opportunity for adventure and intrigue, for new experiences. The two pillars supported a balcony which seemed to guard the entrance with a watchful eye signaling that the door doesn't open to just anyone.

"Incredible!" was Pasteur's first thought when the butler opened the door allowing the trio into the foyer. Standing on the marble floor, he was amazed at the grandeur that greeted them.

Even Galt, who was more pragmatic about their purpose, was impressed by the lavishness that surrounded them. He leaned over and whispered to Pasteur, "I think we have found that Templar's Treasure."

"This might just be paradise John," Pasteur spoke with his mouth still gaping open.

"Well a dreamland for sure," John Galt added.

"I will show you to your rooms Mr. Franklin. Dr. Dick will join you in the dining room at six o'clock for dinner."

Pasteur could hardly believe the sight of the elegant tapestries and fine furnishings that filled the foyer and the rooms that he could get a glimpse of from where he was standing. Pasteur just stood there in awe, drinking in the art, antiques, artifacts, and gilded furnishings. The luxury didn't end there. He could see through one room out a window into one of the many gardens. The garden was filled with statues, tiered fountains, manicured lawns, unique shrubbery, and beautiful flowers. Pasteur had been to the Governor's Palace in Williamsburg and thought that it paled in comparison to the elegance and grandeur at Prestonfield House.

"The dining room is down the hallway here to your left," the butler interrupted Pasteur's thoughts. "Make yourselves at home. You are welcome to wander the house and gardens as you like." Pasteur thought again about the Templar's treasure and thought that surely Dr. Dick must have it hidden somewhere here in Prestonfield House.

"Let us retire to the library," Dr. Dick encouraged after the group had eaten dinner. Pasteur and Galt were not used to such lavish dinners as the one that Dr. Dick bestowed upon them.

As they made their way toward the library, Ben Franklin excused himself only to return moments later with the Kentucky long rifle that George Washington had provided as a gift for Dr. Dick. "I had it inscribed for you Alexander."

"Thank you so much Ben. This is a beauty." Dick held the stock of the rifle up so as to read the inscription, "*To my friend Alexander Dick—Shoot Straight. Ben Franklin.*"

"So, Dr. Dick, you enjoy shooting?" Galt asked.

"Only my enemies!" There was a momentary silence and then the four men laughed in unison.

"Alexander, I must come straight to the point of our trip from the colonies to visit you," Franklin broke in.

"You mean it isn't my natural charm, along with my liquor and my warm hospitality that brought you here? I thought maybe we could continue our long conversations about electricity."

"Well all of that of course Alexander," Franklin agreed. "We are however, in need of money to fight the Brits. Can you help us? Will you help us?"

"Ben, you know how I feel about the Brits," Dick stood up and walked over to a wall where there was hanging a portrait of his great-grandfather, William Dick. "I will help you in whatever way I can."

"Alexander's great grandfather William Dick," Franklin began explaining to Pasteur and Galt, "had once been the richest man in Scotland. He was so wealthy he had even lent six thousand pounds sterling to King James VI."

"Wasn't he the son of Mary Queen of Scots?" Pasteur asked.

"Yes, that is true," Franklin responded. "It was King James VI who wanted to unite the two kingdoms, Scotland and England into one—Great Britain."

"But," Alexander Dick added, "English nobility felt they were superior to the backwards Scots and yet a Scot was now their King. So a plan was hatched to kill off all the prominent Scots in England."

"That's terrible," Galt surmised.

"That plan of course involved Guy Fawkes attempting to blow up King James VI and parliament," Alexander Dick continued.

"Also," Franklin continued, "when Charles the First was going to visit Scotland, an appeal was made to William Dick for funds to help offset the costs. Dick advanced the King one hundred thousand merks. Dick was provided security by way of the King's revenue. When William Dick went to London to see if he could get some repayment, Cromwell had him thrown in prison. All of his property, money, and treasures were seized. William Dick died penniless and starving in prison. His family was destitute. There wasn't even enough money to bury him properly."

"You certainly have motivation to help us," Galt surmised.

"Yes," Pasteur added. "You will be able to get satisfaction by getting your revenge when we send their red lobster coats packing all the way back to England."

"Revenge isn't my only motive," Dr. Dick continued. "I believe that all men are created equal in the eyes of God. I believe that God wants us all to be able to live our life in freedom and pursue what brings us happiness. When we are bound by political powers that take those God-given rights away from us then we have to fight for them and we have to fight for those who are too weak to fight for themselves."

"Jefferson should be here to listen to this," Franklin said. "I knew we could count on you to help us Alexander."

"How do you plan to get all of this money, arms, and supplies past the troops and into the colonies Ben?"

"John and Will here being doctors, I thought that we could ship them in under the guise of medical supplies."

"Possibly some of it, but we will need a much more involved plan than that. We are going to need someone else to receive the shipments, someone who is unknown and undetectable to the British. Someone who is almost invisible"

"Someone like Zachary Owens?" Franklin chuckled.

Franklin and Dick started to chuckle together and then broke out into uncontrolled laughter. Galt and Pasteur looked at each other in confusion.

"Zachary Owens!" Dick repeated.

Galt just had to know. The suspense was killing him, "Who is Zachary Owens."

"Zachary Owens," Franklin answered still laughing, "is nobody."

"He is nobody," Dr. Dick repeated.

Galt and Pasteur were even more puzzled.

"When Alexander was working in England," Franklin began, "he and a group of his doctor friends invented a persona whom they called Zachary Owens."

"Zach never existed," Dick continued, "but we had everyone fooled. When attendance was taken for a function one of us would simply say that Zach had just stepped out or that he would be arriving late. We had invented a look for Zach, a personality, family history and everything."

"They even had him run for elected positions."

"Which he almost won," Dick added.

"It just might work!" Galt added emphatically. "We could set up Zachary Owens as a guest at the Raleigh Tavern in Williamsburg."

"For sure," Pasteur added. "John and I could carry out the hoax and we could store the shipments in safe places throughout the colonies."

"Like the powder magazine," Galt offered with enthusiasm, "right under the governor's nose."

Franklin and Dick glanced at each other and nodded. Franklin stood up and walked over to where Dick was standing. He looked up at the portrait of William Dick hanging on the wall, "What do you think? Will it work?" Franklin asked Alexander Dick but seemingly asking the portrait.

"I think so. I know so."

"Then let's start planning," Ben directed.

"Benjamin," Dick started in a serious tone, "there is a problem. I am constantly being watched."

"The Templar's Treasure?"

Pasteur's ears were tickled when Franklin mentioned the Templar's Treasure.

"Yes, there are many who think that I possess it or know where it is."

"And do you?" Franklin queried.

"Does anyone?" Dick avoided the question.

Pasteur didn't know what to think now. Was Dick just playing along with Franklin or did he really have the Templar's Treasure. Why was he being watched if he didn't know where the treasure was.

"Now that you are here," Dick added, "you will be watched as well."

"I know," Franklin confirmed, "that is why I brought along Will and John here. I thought that perhaps we could introduce them to some of the doctors at the College of Physicians to learn the latest techniques that way those that are watching will believe that we are on a medical learning trip."

"I will need one of them to come with me tomorrow. You take the other to the College of Physicians."

"Which one do you want to go with you?"

Dr. Alexander Dick glanced at Pasteur and then Galt. "I will take Pasteur with me. You can take Galt to the College of Physicians. I will draw up a letter of introduction tonight for you to take with you."

"Thank you Dr. Dick. I am looking forward to meeting some of the staff and instructors at the College," John Galt said.

"You are quite welcome John. We had a recent graduate who I believe is now practicing in Philadelphia."

"Who would that be?" asked Galt.

"His name is Benjamin Rush, a very intelligent fellow. Although, he has some strange ideas about blood-letting."

Franklin spoke up, "I know Dr. Rush. He is a member of the Continental Congress."

"Dr. Rush has some very good qualities," Alexander Dick added. "He believes in treating rich and poor equally. It doesn't matter to him if people can't afford to pay him."

"That is admirable," Franklin said.

"Where are we going tomorrow Dr. Dick?" Pasteur asked.

"It is a secret. Can you keep secrets?"

"Yes. I can."

"Then I will take you to see the Templar's Treasure," Dr. Dick joked.

At hearing that, Franklin choked on his liquor and went into a coughing spasm. Then all of them started laughing. The four men spent the remainder of the evening talking and drinking liquor. Franklin and Dick rehashed old stories and adventures with Galt and Pasteur listening intensely. Especially did Galt and Pasteur enjoy the numerous stories about the adventures of Zachary Owens.

MARY KING'S CLOSE

EDINBURGH, SCOTLAND

1771

About noon the following day, a carriage and driver pulled up in front of Prestonfield House. Will Pasteur and Dr. Alexander Dick climbed up into the carriage along with Dick's son Robert Keith. Dick called up to the driver, "The Castle Hill Pub please."

"Aye sir."

Pasteur thought that it was a little early in the day to be going to a pub and wondered why Dick was bringing along his young son to a pub. This was Pasteur's first visit to Scotland. He didn't talk much during the ride. He was more interested in taking in the local sights along the route. After a short ride, the carriage pulled to a stop in front of Castle Hill Pub.

Castle Hill Pub was unlike any of the taverns that Pasteur was used to back in Williamsburg. It was much older, dirtier, and dilapidated. Upon entering, Pasteur perceived that the patrons themselves were disheveled, dirty and rowdy. He didn't know exactly what he and Dr. Dick were doing here but he put his trust in Dick and didn't ask any questions. Pasteur thought surely the Templar's treasure wasn't here. He wandered toward the bar thinking that they were here to get a drink. Dick and Robert Keith had actually walked in behind the bar. Pasteur watched as Dick lifted up a trap door. He then motioned for Pasteur to follow him. Pasteur was a little confused but thought that this was getting interesting.

They descended down a ladder about fifteen feet to a man made vault of stone. It was dark and damp. Dick reached up to a familiar place and taking a torch lit it. He handed it to Robert Keith. "Follow us," he told Pasteur.

The path they followed was a steady decline, sometimes winding and sometimes straight but always damp and musty smelling. Water was weeping out of the stone walls. As they descended ever deeper into the earth, Pasteur noticed a stench of sewage. They turned a bend and then the path opened into what seemed to be an entire underground town. There were women hanging out laundry, children playing in the roadways which were lit by torches, and merchants of every sort including cobblers, tinsmiths, hat makers, and bakers.

Pasteur had never seen anything like this. People were walking about, talking, carrying on activities that you would normally see above ground. Buildings rose to three stories in places. Pasteur was walking with his jaw hanging open, taking in all of the sights.

"Gardez lieu!" a voice called out from above as one of the underground residents dumped a bucket of human waste out of a window opening.

Dick and Robert Keith jumped aside but some of the bucket's contents hit Pasteur on the sleeve of his overcoat.

Dick chuckled, "Sorry Will. I should have warned you about that."

Pasteur then realized that while he thought they had been walking through a muddy pathway, it was actually a river of sewage, human waste.

Dick continued along the underground road until he came to the door of a pub called Uncle Duncan's. He entered with Pasteur following closely behind. Pasteur was thinking to himself that with all of this mystery of underground caves and tunnels, surely they were heading toward the treasure.

Pasteur was astounded at the atmosphere in Uncle Duncan's. It was filthier and dungier than the Castle Hill Pub. The clientele was even more disheveled and appeared that they hadn't seen the light of day for months. They were drinking, smoking, joking, laughing, singing, playing instruments, and some men and women were engaging in lewd conduct. Pasteur didn't think this was a good atmosphere for Robert Keith to be in and he looked over at Robert Keith to see his reaction. There wasn't any. Robert Keith followed his father through the crowd bidding greetings to familiar faces. Pasteur asked Dick if he thought that it was appropriate for Robert Keith to be here.

"He's got to be carefully taught," Dick explained.

Dr. Dick went through a door at the back of the pub to a large room filled with these underground inhabitants. Their faces and disposition perked up with Dr. Dick's presence. He then passed through a second door into what appeared to be a fully equipped examination room. Robert Keith waited in the larger room and Pasteur followed Dr. Dick.

A moment or two later, Robert Keith helped an old woman to the door of the examination room, "Here is your first patient, Father."

"Hello Mrs. Holland. How can I help you today?"

The old woman obviously had many ailments but she was holding a cloth over her eye and this seemed to be her main concern. "Oh Dr. Dick, I think that I have an infection in my eye," she pleaded.

Dr. Dick removed the cloth and bathed her eye with salve. He provided her with a small glass bottle filled with a remedy of some sort and told her to bathe her eye with it twice each day. Dr. Dick then reached into a cabinet and took out some coins which he gave to the woman. Pasteur had a surprised look on his face. What is this? He thought. Dr. Dick provides medical services and then pays the patient?

Dick knew that this would bring a reaction from Pasteur, "Will, other than my son, you are the only person not from this underground city that knows about this place. These people need medical attention the same as the wealthier people who live above ground. They can't afford to pay. They also need money for food. I believe that we who are privileged need to share the wealth."

Robert Keith appeared at the door again, "Your next patient father."

"He's got to be carefully taught?" Pasteur repeated to Dick.

"That's correct," Dick responded, "he's got to be carefully taught."

Pasteur then jumped in to start helping Dick with one patient after another. The two men worked side by side late into the night. By the time the last patient had been attended to, Robert Keith had already fallen asleep on a bench in the larger room.

Duncan, the pub owner, brought the two men some stew and bread along with a pint of ale. "The young lad has already eaten," he said.

Pasteur and Dick gulped down their ale and finished their food. "We will sleep here tonight," Dick informed as he took three blankets from a chest. He handed one to Pasteur and then went into the other room to put one over Robert Keith. As he put the blanket over the lad, Robert Keith looked up at his father with a smile.

From inside the examining room, Pasteur could over-hear the boy say, "We helped lots today."

"Aye, Robert. That we did. That we did."

The exhausted Pasteur wasn't long falling asleep. As he snuggled the best he could on the floor with his blanket, the odor of the sewage only became a faint memory to him. He was getting used to it. He also wondered who this strange man was, this doctor to the needy, this Alexander Dick.

Morning came too early as far as Pasteur was concerned. Dick brought some coffee and bread into the examining room, "Eat Will. You will need your strength today."

"Are we seeing more patients?" Pasteur asked.

"Not today. Today we look after my friend Franklin's needs."

Dr. Dick, Will, and Robert Keith left Uncle Duncan's pub and continued making their way through the underground city. It seemed that almost every person who they passed on the underground streets knew Dr. Dick. They would wave or nod to him. It was obvious to Pasteur that Dr. Dick was well respected by the underground inhabitants.

"By now," Alexander Dick told Pasteur, "we are beneath the Royal Mile. As far as the people who live in the city above believe, this area below is a den of thieves and drunkards. There is nothing but brothels and pubs, thieves and cutthroats. Even the constables are afraid to come down here."

"And you Dr. Dick? Are you not afraid?"

"These people trust me. I look after their needs and they help me with my businesses. I am honest with them and loyal. They are the same in return."

Alexander Dick stopped and turned in at an arch in the wall that appeared to be an underground vault in the underground city. He rapped on a stone with his cane. Suddenly a portion of stone wall moved aside exposing a doorway into a large hall with a beehive of activity going on. A very large, scruffy-looking man blocked the doorway. Upon seeing Dr. Dick, the man automatically stepped aside to let him pass. Then he stepped back in front of Pasteur.

"It's alright McCafferty, Will is a friend."

McCafferty allowed Pasteur to pass. "Dr. Dick that William Brodie fella showed up here again yesterday. Doin' some snoopin' around he was."

"Thanks McCafferty. Keep your eye on him. I don't trust that one."

"Who is Brodie, Father?" young Robert Keith asked.

"William Brodie sits on the Edinburgh Town Council. He is also a deacon of the Incorporation of Wrights and Masons. I get a bad feeling about him and that group he hangs around with—Brown, Ainslie, and that Mr. Smith."

Pasteur could see that there was quite an operation going on. On one side of the hall was a distillery with at least twenty people working. On the other side of the hall carpenters were making caskets. The spirits so to speak were being placed in the caskets which were then stacked at the far end of the hall.

"This is what is known as an underground distillery Will. Yes, it is illegal, but it avoids paying lofty taxes to the Brits and then I use the funds to help those who truly need it. We ship the liquor out in caskets as everyone above ground thinks the plague is still going on down here and they won't go near a casket that is brought out from the vaults."

"So is this where the Dick family fortune comes from?" Will asked.

"In part. I have many businesses that add to my good fortune."

"Here I was thinking that all of the wealth at Prestonfield House must surely be from the Templar's Treasure," Will expressed disappointedly.

"Come with me Will."

Dick walked to the back of the hall where the caskets were stacked. After getting Will to help him move a few of the caskets, Dick now had access to a large locked door. He unlocked the door and entered. Lighting a torch, Dick motioned Will to enter. Will could not believe his eyes. There were several chests overflowing with gold and silver coins. Gold and silver trinkets and chalices were piled up almost covering the entire floor space. There were gems and treasures of every sort.

"My goodness! It's true! The Templar's Treasure!"

Dick burst out in laughter, "This isn't the Templar's Treasure. This is the Dick family treasure. This is what is going to help Benjamin Franklin finance his fight with Britain."

"Where did you get all this?"

Dick motioned back towards the distillery.

Dick walked over to one small chest. He opened it and took out something wrapped in an old, soiled linen cloth. Dick carefully unwrapped the cloth revealing a chalice which he held up to the light of the torch. "What do you see here Will?" he asked.

"It's a chalice, a pewter chalice. Although, it isn't made of silver or gold like these others. It's actually more like an old cup."

"This, young Will, is the Holy Grail."

"No it couldn't be! The grail is part of the Templar's Treasure."

"Yes Will, that is true, and I am the guardian of that treasure. My family has been the guardian of the Templar's Treasure for over two hundred years now. That is one of the reasons that my great-grandfather William Dick was thrown into prison by Cromwell. Cromwell was trying to get it out of my great-grandfather where the treasure was hidden."

"So where is it?" Will asked hoping for an answer but not really expecting one.

"Come further into the catacombs with me Will," Dick walked to the back of the vault and then unlocked another door. This door led to another vault much larger than the first. "Will, behind this door lies the Templar's Treasure. You will be one of the few in modern times to see it. You must not tell anyone that it is here. Do you promise?"

"Yes, I promise."

Dr. Dick unlocked the door and pushed it open. Stepping in, he lit a torch.

"My goodness! This is magnificent! Unbelievable!" The vault was filled with ancient artifacts of gold and silver. There were jewels and gems overflowing. Old coins, diamonds, and rubies filled chests which in turn filled the vault. "Does Ben Franklin know this is here?"

"Benjamin knows that my family is protecting the treasure and has knowledge of its whereabouts. But he has never seen this vault. Outside of my family, you are the only one to be present here."

Still awestruck by all of the wealth that surrounded him, Will asked, "Why show this to me? Why now?"

"Because," Dick, sounding discouraged, continued, "I am getting old. Hiding this treasure has been a burden on my family. My great-grandfather William Dick lost his life to Cromwell because of trying to protect this treasure. This is a burden that I don't want to pass along to my son. It is time to move the treasure to the new world. The Freemasons can look after it themselves. You and Franklin and Galt are going to help me. In exchange, I will give Franklin the money he needs, from my own resources, to finance the war with the British. I had to bring you here so that you can verify that the treasure is here. Also, if anything happens to me while

I am trying to get the treasure moved, someone else will know where to find it"

"Dr. Dick, this is an honor that I don't deserve," Pasteur said humbly.

"Will, I discussed this with Franklin last night. He said you are trustworthy and loyal. If you do misplace my trust then I have friends in the colonies who will kill you." Dick was still holding the grail. "I want you to take this back to Williamsburg with you."

"What am I to do with it? Surely a relic like this won't be safe. Shouldn't it be in some sanctuary somewhere where it can be venerated?"

"It is just a relic. It is not to be venerated or worshiped. Remember the Bible tells us that we are to worship our God Yahweh alone. We are not to worship any idols."

"So why do you have this?"

"To protect true worship from those who would venerate it. Being the cup that Christ used, false religious leaders would make all kinds of claims about it having magical healing powers."

"Does it?" Will asked.

"No, not at all. It is just a cup. There are those who would exploit it for their own purposes."

"So what am I to do with it?" Will asked.

"Hide it in plain sight."

"How do I do that?"

"When you return, set it right on a shelf in your apothecary. Nobody will even suspect that it is actually the Holy Grail. Will—there is something more that I want you to do for me. I want you to take my son Robert Keith and my daughter Anne to the colonies with you. I have a friend in Charles Towne, William Bull is his name. His son is also a medical doctor. Robert Keith and Anne can stay with Mr. and Mrs. Bull."

"It would be a pleasure Dr. Dick."

Before Franklin, Galt, and Pasteur headed back to Yorktown along with young Robert Keith Dick and Anne Dick in tow, Dr. Alexander Dick called his son to his side. "Robert Keith," he started.

"Yes Father."

"As you know, I am sending you and your sister Anne to Charles Towne and I am going to supply the money, arms, and supplies that the colonies need to fight against the Brits. That will come out of our family fortune."

"Yes Father, I know that. I understand."

"There will be more than enough for the colonists to fight their war and you and your sister are to keep some of it for you to establish a new life for yourselves when the war is over," Dr. Dick explained to young Robert Keith who was listening intently. "Son, I do trust these men. Benjamin Franklin and I have been friends for many years. I will be sending the Templar's treasure to the colonies as well. That is not to be used for the war. I want you to write in this log book here," Dr. Dick emphasized, handing his young son a leather-bound book, "as ships come in. You are to record when the ship arrives and what is contained in the shipment. Also we will need to hide the contents straight away. It is important that you record where the contents have been taken to be hidden."

"But how will I know Father?"

"McCafferty and some of his close friends from the underground will disguise themselves as pirates and allow themselves to be caught. It is already being arranged that they will be put in prison in the lower level of the Exchange. McCafferty will provide you with a list of each shipment. He will oversee the contents as they arrive in port."

"How will he do that Father if he is in prison?"

"That has all been arranged as well. You will get further instructions in Charles Towne. Also, you are to keep Mr. Franklin informed as to the locations where the Templar's Treasure has been hidden."

"And what of our family fortune, Father?" Robert Keith asked.

"You must keep Dr. Pasteur and Dr. Galt informed so that they can dispense what is needed when it is needed," Dr. Alexander Dick responded to his son.

"Father, how will I know when your ships arrive?"

"I will have three horsemen painted on the main sail. When you see those horsemen on a ship entering the harbor, you will know that it is one of my ships."

"But Father, I don't want to go."

"Aye, I know son. You are who I trust the most."

"But Father, you trust McCafferty and his men. Can't they do this and I stay here at Prestonfield House with you?"

"You and your sister are my greatest treasure. You are worth more to me than our family fortune or the Templar's treasure. Benjamin Franklin,

Dr. Pasteur, and Dr. Galt have promised to keep what I am doing for them a secret. My name is not to be associated with this war at all. Nor am I to be attributed with contributing or helping with anything. That is our agreement. But if it is found out that I have helped the colonists there may be dire consequences. I could be tried for treason and put to death. I want you and your sister safely away in the new world where you can make a new life for yourselves. You will accomplish great things, Robert Keith. You have been carefully taught."

THE APOTHECARY AT
WILLIAMSBURG

1772

"So, how do you know all of this Jack," Bill asked.

"I can see how you may be wondering how Jacques Pierre Falstaff an Australian with a French Canadian mother got to know so much about the Dick family treasure and all of the goings on that occurred in 1771 Charleston," Jack acknowledged. "Well, although I have been raised in Australia, my ancestors were Canadian. Several generations of the Falstaff family had lived in Nova Scotia, Canada. They too had their stories that were passed on from generation to generation and eventually landed on my ears as a youth," Jack continued.

Will Pasteur and John Galt arranged for a room to be booked at the Raleigh Tavern under the name of Zachary Owens. Galt explained to Henry Wetherburn, the Tavern's owner, that Mr. Owens was an itinerant artist from Scotland whom he and Pasteur had met while recently in Scotland with Benjamin Franklin. Galt explained to Mr. Wetherburn that he may not see Mr. Owens much but that there would be many deliveries in the name of Zachary Owens as he was having many of his works and family heirlooms shipped over from Edinburgh. Pasteur and Galt arranged that all payments for the room would be done through them and that when Mr. Owens was in his room, he was not to be disturbed.

The room was a private one with a single bed, a wash stand, dresser, writing desk, and a couple of high-back wooden chairs. Galt procured some artist's supplies and a half-finished painting which he staged on the writing desk as if a painter was working and had just stepped out of the room.

Pasteur arranged at the post office for them to inform him when anything arrived for Zachary Owens and he would pay for and accept the package or shipment.

"Your friend, Owens is very elusive Dr. Pasteur," claimed Henry Wetherburn one evening when Dr. Pasteur and Dr. Galt visited the Raleigh Tavern to play some billiards, have a meal and drink some flip.

"You are correct there Mr. Wetherburn," Dr. Pasteur responded. "Dr. Galt and myself rarely see that Scotsman. Although, I do understand that he has been commissioned by some very prominent people to create some paintings. I should go up and see if he would like to join us for dinner." A few minutes later, Pasteur returned. "Mr. Owens doesn't care to join us for dinner as he is busy but he asked if you could send a meal up to his room. He asked that Dr. Galt bring the meal up as he has some business to conduct with Dr. Galt."

"I will get his meal prepared," Henry Wetherburn answered.

Dr. Galt and Dr. Pasteur simply grinned at each other. "Thank you," Dr. Pasteur said.

As the evening rolled on, Dr. Galt took the meal up to Zachary Owens' room and sat down and ate it. He returned down to the public dining room with the empty dishes then joined his friend Dr. Pasteur playing some more billiards. "Mr. Owens enjoyed that greatly, Mr. Wetherburn. He said to pass along his thanks."

"Let Mr. Owens know that he is welcome anytime."

Steadily, packages, letters, and larger containers arrived in Williamsburg for Zachary Owens. Dr. Pasteur or Dr. Galt would pick them up, pay for them and then take them to their apothecaries. Although tensions were heating up between the Colonists and the British, there was no immediate need for the Colonists to use what Dr. Alexander Dick was shipping them from Scotland. So Dr. Pasteur and Dr. Galt were stockpiling the arms, supplies, medical supplies, money, and the Dick family treasure and the Templar's treasure. They hid some items in the powder magazine and guardhouse. Some items were kept in the apothecaries themselves, and other items were hidden at various locations in and around the countryside of Williamsburg. Robert Keith Dick would send letters to Zachary Owens, in order to notify Dr. Pasteur and Dr. Galt what had arrived in Charleston.

Dr. Pasteur had an assistant in his apothecary. His name was Frederick Falstaff. Falstaff was a very rugged looking man. He was handsome to the ladies and very well liked by many in Williamsburg. Dr. Pasteur liked Falstaff as well and trusted him immensely. One day, Pasteur, upon returning to his apothecary, found Falstaff standing by the window. Falstaff had just come in from the outside himself as he still was wearing his three-cornered hat. Falstaff was very focused on an object that he was holding. His hair was tied back. There were other objects strewn about Dr. Pasteur's desk.

Frederick Falstaff

"What have you there, Mr. Falstaff?" Dr. Pasteur asked as he entered the examining room at his apothecary.

"I am not completely sure Dr. Pasteur," answered Falstaff. "I was at the post office and printer when the post master gave me this package for you. It said medical supplies so I opened it. But I discovered that these items are not medical supplies at all. Upon examining the package further I noticed that it was actually for a Mr. Zachary Owens. Isn't Mr. Owens your friend who is staying at the Raleigh Tavern?"

"Indeed he is."

"I wonder what he is up to?"

"How so?" Pasteur asked.

"Well these items are very rare and extremely valuable. This item in particular," Falstaff continued, "is said to have been part of the Templar's Treasure."

Dr. Pasteur reasoned that he had better bring Frederick Falstaff in on their scheme. After all, Falstaff had been Dr. Pasteur's loyal and faithful assistant for a number of years. Yet, he didn't expose all of the details of the plan. For Dr. Pasteur knew that even trusted friends could turn in these treacherous times. "Falstaff, Mr. Owens is helping Dr. Galt and I to build up supplies and arms in case the Colonists engage the British in war."

"But, Dr. Pasteur, that is treason!"

"To some it is treason. To others it is fighting for our freedom."

"But what of these items Dr. Pasteur? These are not items of war. These are treasures."

"Yes that is true. And you are correct. These items are part of the Templar's Treasure. When Dr. Galt and I were in Scotland, Benjamin Franklin introduced us to a Dr. Alexander Dick who has been safeguarding the Templar's Treasure. Dr. Dick has been shipping the treasure to Zachary Owens for safekeeping here in the colony."

"That is amazing Dr. Pasteur. But where is it being kept?"

There are levels of trust that humans have with each other. One may trust their spouse with their most guarded secrets. One may trust their neighbor with less. There are some things that are only kept between man and God. When Falstaff asked this question of Dr. Pasteur, Dr. Pasteur thought about all of the people involved in putting together this scheme and how it could be derailed by loose lips or worse yet, traitorous lips. He thought that he could trust Falstaff, but exactly how much could he trust him? Dr. Pasteur had noticed an ambitious spirit in Falstaff and thought what if Falstaff used this information to get rid of Pasteur and take over his practice? No, Dr. Pasteur thought, he was likely just being paranoid. Glancing down, he noticed the return address on the package as 35 Meeting Street.

"37 Meeting Street," Dr. Pasteur answered. "Some of the treasure is being kept at 37 Meeting Street in Charleston."

"And the rest?"

"I have stowed it in places in and around Williamsburg. Some of it is right here in the apothecary."

"This is amazing Dr. Pasteur."

That evening Dr. Pasteur met Dr. Galt at the Raleigh Tavern and explained the situation that had happened earlier that day. "I don't like it Will," Dr. Galt expressed.

"I can trust Falstaff."

"I am not so sure about that Will. I have heard that Falstaff actually sympathizes with the British. Did you know that he is fond of the daughter of a British officer?"

"No. I didn't know that."

"From what I have heard from some of the brothers is that he acts so honest and upright when he is with you but he deals treacherously with others. Some say that you are blind to his actions."

"I tell you John, I can trust him. He would never do anything to harm me and my family." Even though Pasteur was saying these words he started to have doubts in his mind, wondering if he had made the right decision to share information with Falstaff. But then Pasteur thought if he hadn't then Falstaff may have exposed Zachary Owens as Falstaff had already found what he believed to be items from the Templar's Treasure in the package addressed to Owens.

Frederick Falstaff had started to keep track of packages coming for Zachary Owens and the occasions when Dr. Pasteur or Dr. Galt would pick up these packages. He would follow Dr. Pasteur into the countryside to the neighboring towns and villages and make notes of where he believed that items were being hidden.

"You are certain about this Mr. Falstaff?" the governor questioned.

"Yes Your Worship. He said the treasure is hidden at 37 Meeting Street in Charleston." Falstaff had reasoned that if he could help the British by exposing Dr. Pasteur's scheme and help them find all of the hidden treasure and supplies that the Colonists were storing up then he could win some points with the father of the girl who he was in love with.

"That is where General Howe is staying. I will have to get word to him to search that house from top to bottom. Son you don't know how much this information will be appreciated. Are you interested in being conscripted to spy for the British?"

"Yes sir. That would be an honor."

"Then continue to watch Dr. Pasteur and Dr. Galt and advise us of any packages of so-called medical supplies that arrive for this Zachary Owens."

There was a loud knocking on the door of Dr. Pasteur's apothecary. "Dr Pasteur, Dr. Pasteur."

"Yes, yes, what is it?" Dr. Pasteur called out as he descended the stairs to answer the door. He had already been in bed sleeping. "Henry Wetherburn, what are you doing here this hour of the night?"

"It's your assistant Frederick Falstaff."

"Is he okay? Has he been hurt?"

"He is fine. He will be a little hung-over in the morning. Mr. Falstaff was at the Raleigh Tavern tonight. He was drinking quite heavy. I overheard him telling some men who he was drinking with that he was hired by the governor to spy on you and that Zachary Owens was having treasure shipped from Scotland."

"I see."

"I have suspected for a while now that there was something out of the ordinary with Mr. Owens. I don't know what you and Dr. Galt are up to but I am sure that whatever it is, it is to help the Colony. I don't want to see your plan undermined. So I thought that you had better know about this."

"Thank you Mr. Wetherburn. This is very important. Would you wait a moment while I write a note?"

"Yes, Dr. Pasteur."

A few minutes later, Dr. Pasteur handed a note to Henry Wetherburn, "Please see that Benjamin Franklin gets this. This is very urgent."

"Yes, Dr. Pasteur. I will."

A few days later

"Falstaff, will you come in here a moment?" Dr. Pasteur called out from the examination room to Falstaff, who was in the front room of the apothecary.

"What is it Dr. Pasteur?" Falstaff asked as he entered the examination room. His jaw dropped in surprise and shock as he saw not only Dr. Pasteur but also Dr. Galt and Benjamin Franklin.

"We know that you are a spy for the British Mr. Falstaff," Benjamin Franklin stated quite bluntly.

"What have you told them," Dr. Galt demanded

"Surely, you don't think that I am going to tell you."

"You don't have to tell us. You remember what happened last week to poor Mrs. Randolph when the townsfolk found out that her and her husband were sympathizers of the British? They were going to tar and feather her."

Pasteur, bring me one of your tooth extracting instruments," Galt requested. When Pasteur returned with the instrument, Galt told Franklin and Pasteur to hold Falstaff down. "I'm going to pull your teeth out," Galt said.

"You don't scare me."

"Wait," Franklin ordered. "We don't need to hurt him. Henry!" Franklin called down to the cold cellar.

Henry Wetherburn stuck his head out of the cold cellar looking up the stairs. He had a young woman with him. "Frederick," she cried out.

"Margaret!" Falstaff answered, seeing the girl who he was in love with. "Don't you dare harm her!"

"Now do you want to tell us what you have told the governor?" Benjamin Franklin asked.

"As long as you promise not to harm my Margaret."

"Tell us," Dr. Galt demanded.

"I told the governor that Zachary Owens was bringing treasure, arms and supplies in from Scotland and that you and Dr. Pasteur were hiding the items in Williamsburg and in nearby towns and villages. I also told him that some of the treasure was hidden at 37 Meeting Street in Charleston."

"Well Mr. Falstaff, we are going to make you the deal of a lifetime," Dr. Galt started. "We can either turn you over to some of the Colonists as a spy and let them deal with you or you can voluntarily leave the country with your lovely Margaret and never return."

"Where will I go? I can't go to England. They will throw me in the stockade."

"Mr. Franklin owns a great deal of property in Nova Scotia, as does the Dick family," Dr. Galt continued. "We will have some people escort you and Margaret there. Mr. Franklin will prepare documents to transfer a small piece of property for you and Margaret to reside on the mainland near Oak Island. In return, you will help us hide some of the treasure in parts of Canada and on Oak Island. So long as you do what we say, you and Margaret will be able to live your life out in peace. If you double-cross us then you will lose your property and we will come after the both of you."

"I accept your offer. Dr. Pasteur."

THE EDMONDSTON-ALSTON HOUSE

CHARLESTON

MAY 1976

"Well Jack, that certainly is quite a story. Now I can see why they call you Bull Scat Jack." Bill joked.

"I told you," Fripp piped up from behind the bar.

"It's true," Jack claimed. "I can prove it."

"So my ancestors financed the American Revolution and had possession of the Templar's Treasure. You're not just Bull Scat Jack, you're Crazy Jack."

"I can prove it. I will prove it," Jack defended.

"How?" Bill asked not expecting a believable answer. He was actually enjoying getting Jack riled up.

"Meet me tomorrow at noon in front of 21 East Battery."

"Can I come too?" Fripp asked, not wanting to be left out.

"Sure. The more the merrier," Jack replied.

"I wouldn't miss this for all the tea in the Boston Harbor," Fripp quipped.

Bill stood waiting across the road from 21 East Battery. He leaned on the break wall enjoying the gentle ocean breeze. Thoughts of yesterday filled his head, he couldn't stop going over the breakup in his mind. He kept picturing Erica as she got into her car, the last glimpse he had of her as she weakly waved goodbye. Feelings of sadness overcame him. He had an awful feeling in the pit of his stomach. Turning his face toward the majestic homes on East Battery, and leaning back on the railing at the break wall, he thought that they should be seeing this together. This was her dream. Erica had often talked about seeing the beautiful gardens, walled courtyards, and intricate iron works that framed the magnificent residences. She spoke about taking tours of the historic homes and plantations. Bill felt that his whole world had ended. All of this beauty that surrounded him now meant nothing to him without her.

Bill's self-consuming thoughts were interrupted by some children laughing as they walked by with their parents. His thoughts then turned to Jack and the story he had told him. It was totally impossible that any of what Jack said was true. Yet, he hoped in some way it was true. It was exciting to think that he may have such ties to significant events and such famous people in history. But why had he never heard about any of this before? And if it was true, he wanted to share it with Erica.

Fripp made his way south on East Bay Street and then limped down East Battery. "I knew he wouldn't show up," he called out when he got within earshot of Bill. "That no good story teller."

No sooner had Fripp got those words out of his mouth when a horse drawn carriage approached from South Battery and stopped directly in front of 21 East Battery. "Good day mates," Jack chirped. "Thanks for the lift mate," he acknowledged to the driver as he stepped down from the carriage.

"You're late," Fripp informed.

"Sorry mates. I had to procure some tickets for us."

"Tickets to what?" Fripp asked.

Jack pointed across the road toward 21 East Battery. "To the Edmondston-Alston House," Jack replied. "Therein lays the proof that my story is true."

The men crossed East Battery. Bill noticed the Wisteria growing in the courtyard. It was Erica's favorite. Again a feeling of depression came over him. Once inside, a guide took their tickets and told them that the tour would begin shortly. Jack and Fripp looked at pictures and antiques in the foyer while Bill was reading information brochures.

The tour guide started, "The Edmondston—Alston House was built by Charles Edmondston, a Scottish shipping merchant, in 1825. Mr. Edmondston came from the Shetland Islands in Scotland. Here in Charleston, he was a local merchant and also owned one of the wharfs." The tour group walked into the parlor as she continued, "In 1838 Charles

Alston purchased the house. He added the Greek Revival features including the third level piazza and the roof parapet."

After touring the first floor, the group ascended a large staircase. At the top of the staircase, a library was situated to the left. The hallway continued straight ahead where it opened onto a piazza. On either side of the hallway were parlors where the family did their entertaining. The tour group entered the library. The guide commented, "The rifle above the fireplace is believed to have once been owned by George Washington himself. There is a plaque by the rifle that says this. The rifle was given as a gift to a Scottish aristocrat who then gave it as a gift to the Edmondston family who had done some shipping of the aristocrat's family's belongings to the colonies. When Charles Edmondston moved to Charleston from the Shetland Islands in Scotland, he brought the rifle with him."

Moving on to the parlors and then out onto the piazza, "General Pierre G. T. Beauregard stood upon this piazza," she continued, "as the first shots were fired on Fort Sumter at the start of the Civil War."

"You see," Jack whispered. "That's the gun that Ben Franklin gave to your ancestor."

"I don't see squat," Fripp cut in. "Just cause that tour guide said that rifle might have been owned by George Washington don't prove nuthin."

The group moved from the piazza to view another chamber room on the second floor. Before anyone realized what was happening, Jack grabbed the rifle from the library, and was examining it out on the piazza. "Sir, what are you doing?" the guide said alarmed.

A tall magnolia tree stood just inside the garden wall, its branches extending upwards past the second floor piazza. Jack, still clutching the rifle, leapt over the railing and climbed down the magnolia tree. Fripp and Bill looked at each other in shock. Almost simultaneously they realized that they were now considered accessories to Jack's antics. They looked to escape and bolted down the stairs, Bill helping Fripp along so that they could go faster. They tripped and almost fell on the bottom step—the one that the guide had warned them was shorter than the others. Once outside, Fripp and Bill didn't know where Jack went but their immediate concern was to not get caught themselves. They headed north on East Battery and ducked into back lanes as they worked their way back to the Alvermay.

Later that night Jack showed up at the Alvermay. Fripp and Bill were still a bit shaken.

"You're crazy," Fripp scolded. "What were you thinking? There are two ways to gain fame in Charleston. One is to do something incredibly heroic. The second is to do something incredibly stupid. You have just proved how stupid you are."

"I wanted to prove to you that my story's true. Come out back with me for a minute."

Fripp and Bill went with Jack through the kitchen and out the rear door to the alley. Jack led them over to a group of garbage cans and reaching behind, he produced the rifle.

"Here Bill," Jack offered. "It's yours. It belongs to you. Look at the part of the stock that was facing the wall when it was hanging above the fireplace. There is a carved inscription that you couldn't read."

Bill held the gun up to see better. Although it was quite worn, he could make out the words. "*To my friend Alexander Dick—Shoot Straight. Ben Franklin.*"

"This is amazing!" Bill exclaimed. "But it's stolen."

"That's not the only problem," Jack added. "The news says the police are looking for a William Dick from Toronto."

"What?" Fripp questioned. "How could the police possibly know that Bill was with you?"

"I signed the guestbook," Bill offered sheepishly.

"You idiot," Fripp scolded.

"How was I supposed to know that Jack was going to steal this relic?"

"The kid is right Fripp. He hasn't hung around me as long as you have. Nor did he realize that I would steal this silver candlestick. I couldn't manage to get the pair though. We better hide the gun. How about in the kitchen storage room?"

"We are going to have to get Bill a new identity," Fripp said. I have a friend that we can go see tomorrow."

Back inside, Jack and Bill sat at the bar while Fripp looked after customers. "So now do you believe me?" Jack asked Bill.

"I guess I have no choice. But is the whole story true?"

"To the best of my knowledge mate."

"Then," Bill was thinking out loud, "there might be some of the treasure here in Charleston?"

"It's possible Bill," Jack answered. "There's a legend that there was pirate's treasure buried at 37 Meeting Street. Maybe it was actually the treasure that your ancestor sent over from Scotland. The British took control of the house during the revolution and completely plundered the place. Obviously they believed that there was something hidden there. But I would imagine that if there had been any treasure, the British found it and took it."

"Unless," Bill mused, "it never was there. Maybe it was somewhere else."

That night Bill lay awake in his room. It was extremely hot even for the people in Charleston, let alone a fellow from Toronto. The window was open allowing the noise of the traffic on East Bay Street to fill the room. Yet even with the window open, there wasn't much air movement. Bill was thinking about Erica again. How could she do that to him? They were best friends. They had shared so many memories together—pulling all-nighters studying for exams, family moments when her father was really ill, partying, long walks, talking into the wee hours of the morning about life, and of course the romantic moments. He wanted her here with him now. He didn't care how many guys she had cheated on him with, he loved her and missed her. Bill had never really understood what an aching heart was until now.

As the night wore on, traffic on East Bay died down so that there was only the occasional car. Every time a car would travel north past the Alvermay, the car's headlights would reflect on the north wall of Bill's room. The reflection was like a welcome visitor. It would shine on the north wall and then as the vehicle continued north, the reflection would move across the north wall towards the east. It would transfer to the east wall as the vehicle was almost at the hotel. The light would then travel south along the east wall and then as the vehicle passed Bill's room, the light would disappear—just as silently and as quietly as it had appeared.

Bill called the light "the Quiet Light." "Hello friend," Bill would say. "Thanks for keeping me company."

Bill's life had sure taken a one hundred and eighty degree turn. He was supposed to be enjoying the summer with Erica and here he was sleeping in a dumpy hotel room by himself and he was wanted by the police. He could hear a drunk talking to himself from the next room.

Every now and then the drunk would start yelling, this coupled with the heat made it practically impossible for Bill to fall asleep.

The room on the other side of Bill's was occupied by a prostitute. He could hear practically every sound coming from the very obvious lovemaking. Although he tried to ignore it to give the couple their privacy, there was no use. Bill wondered if Jack was having as hard a time falling asleep in his room across the hall. To occupy his mind he continued to watch and wait for the Quiet Light.

Bill could hear some commotion out in the hallway and then there was a soft knock on the door, "Are you awake?" A female's voice came from the other side of the door. "Can I come in?"

"Who is it?" Bill asked.

"It's Kitty Gartrell, from the next room."

The prostitute?! Bill thought. I don't want anything to do with a prostitute.

"Can I come in? I can't sleep. It's far too hot."

"Fine, come in. The door isn't locked."

Kitty entered Bill's room wearing her bra and panties and a very loose fitting silk robe which she hadn't bothered to fasten. She was smoking a cigarette and had a couple of ice cold beers in her hand. Closing the door behind her she sauntered over and sat down on the edge of Bill's bed.

"Look miss, I don't go for paying prostitutes for sex," Bill warned with a worried voice.

Kitty laughed. "Don't worry son. I just need some company, just want to talk. What's your name son?"

"Bill."

"And I'm Kitty. My real name's Katarina Gartrelli. Kitty Gartrell is my stage name. I used to be a singer with a blues band so I used that as my stage name and most folks know me by that name." Bill thought that she suited her name. Her voice was raspy from cigarettes and whiskey.

As they talked through the night, Bill learned that Kitty had once been a Playboy bunny and then had a thriving career as a blues singer in the night clubs in the French Quarter. Now as her looks and voice were fading, she made her permanent residence at the Alvermay where Fripp would look the other way to her using his establishment to pick up johns.

Finally at some time during the night, Kitty went back to her room and Bill fell asleep. Perhaps the Quiet Light had comforted him and provided him the power and fortitude to ignore his circumstances.

"C'mon Bill. We gotta get movin'. We gotta get you outa here," Fripp was banging on the door. Fripp entered, "The police were here last night asking me if I knew you."

"Wha . . . What? What are you talking about Fripp?"

"They heard that the guy who stole the gun from the Edmondston Alston House was with a black man with a gimp leg. So naturally, a lot of people know that I fit that description."

Bill hadn't unpacked his clothes and gear so he was pretty much ready to go. He quickly dressed himself and he and Fripp dashed down the stairway, through the kitchen and went out to the back alley. Fripp motioned toward a 1967 Camaro. Bill opened the passenger door and threw his gear in the back.

"Wait Fripp!" Bill said breathlessly. He ran back into the hotel and returned a moment later with the gun. "I'm not leaving this now," he said with a smile. "Where are we going?"

"My wife has an inn on Fripp Island near St. Helena."

"Your wife? You didn't mention you had a wife."

"Louanne doesn't like the city," Fripp explained, "so she runs the Blue Dolphin Inn on the island and I run the Alvermay Hotel here in Charleston."

As Fripp peeled out of the back alley and onto East Bay Street, Bill nodded in approval, "Nice car Fripp!"

"I like it Bill. It goes like spit."

As they made their way toward St. Helena, Fripp asked, "What did you mean Bill when you said that maybe the treasure never was at 37 Meeting Street?"

"Well, I was thinking what if Dr. Dick actually did send the shipments of treasure like Jack said and it was purposely leaked to the British that the treasure was being stored at 37 Meeting Street to throw them off the real location?"

"Then where would it be?" Fripp wondered out loud.

"Somewhere nearby I suppose," Bill offered. "It may have even been in plain sight of the British so that they were unknowingly protecting it. It could possibly be in a house that is very close to or visible from 37 Meeting Street. We need to figure out which one."

"Why?" Fripp asked.

"Why? There could be treasure out there worth millions of dollars. Maybe even more!"

"You don't plan on taking it do you?" Fripp asked, disapprovingly.

"Maybe, maybe not. But—I just need to know," Bill consoled. "It's like I'm on the verge of tying my own life to my ancestors and proof of that treasure is the key. It's like I am suddenly at some crossroad."

"What if we do find it Bill?"

"I don't know Fripp. We both could use some money," Bill chuckled.

"But it doesn't belong to us," Fripp cautioned.

"In a way Fripp, it might belong to me," Bill justified.

"Well son, that's a stretch. If Jack's story is true, it was given up by your ancestor to support the Revolutionary War and therefore it doesn't belong to you."

"Let's worry about it then, if we find it Fripp."

"Deal."

"Can you help me to do some research over the next few days to see if we can narrow down the houses in the area to a short list?" Bill asked.

"Sure. What do you want me to look for?"

"First," explained Bill, "the house has to have been in existence at the time of the Revolutionary War. There also has to be something unique about the house or its occupants."

Fripp continued driving down Highway 21 toward Beaufort. He turned on the radio. It was part way through Paul Simon's song Fifty Ways to Leave Your Lover. " . . . *You slip out the back Jack, make a little plan Stan, just drop off the key Lee, and set yourself free . . .*" Bill thought about Erica again, but only for a moment, his head was spinning with new thoughts, thoughts of treasure. Was it really there? What would they do with it if they found it? Was Bull Scat Jack just spreading more bull scat?

Both men sat in silence the rest of the trip. Clearly Fripp was lost in the same thoughts as Bill.

The Blue Dolphin Inn

Fripp Island

May and June 1976

F ripp turned down the lane at the sign "Blue Dolphin Inn". The sign informed potential guests of its services: *"Waterfront Cottages—daily, weekly, & monthly rates—Established 1856"*.

The laneway leading to the Blue Dolphin Inn wound through a stand of live oak trees which were draped with Spanish moss. It was a breathtaking scene, Bill felt. The main cottage was a two-story Victorian style with an inviting porch on the front and a wrap-around porch on the back. Several smaller cottages were visible in the wood stand. They were low country, cape-cod style. Some were in need of painting and repair. However, they all had the nostalgic look that would captivate the hearts and minds of those interested in South Carolina's by-gone eras. The ocean was visible in the background and when Fripp stopped the car, Bill could hear the waves hitting the shore. The odor of the salt water drifted up through the live oaks capturing Bill's attention and momentarily took him back to when he would go to the beach with his parents and siblings. As his eyes scanned over the scenery before him he couldn`t help but think that this was a place he and Erica used to talk about staying at. They had spent long hours discussing and describing an inn just like this one, with century old trees sweeping over pathways between the cottages and a beach not so far off that you could look out on it from your front porch. These details they had imagined were coming to life before him and he cringed a little at the thought that he was seeing this without her.

There were rocking chairs on each of the cottage porches. They had said they would spend every sunrise and sunset out on the porch, rocking with coffee in hand in the morning and tea at night. Just thinking about this, Bill could taste the coffee in his mouth. Erica would sit and listen to the water while he would sketch or draw or paint whatever inspired him in their surroundings.

It certainly was beautiful. The buildings, although clearly aged and somewhat run down, had a whimsy to them. They wore their history well, and seemed to hold their past and the stories that were part of it as a badge of honor. As he breathed in, he could smell every BBQ, every campfire, every sweet smell of summers gone by all in one breath. He liked this place already.

Blue Dolphin Inn, Fripp Island

"Bill, this is my wife Louanne. Louanne, this is Bill. He is going to be staying here for a few days with you and Sienna while I look after some business in Charleston. Please make him feel at home."

"Welcome Bill," Louanne gestured. "Please make yourself at home. Be comfortable." Louanne was a very striking woman, not at all what Bill expected Fripp's wife to look like. She was white, with long, curly, fiery red hair. Louanne had been born in Ireland and still spoke with a bit of an Irish accent.

"So Louanne, I noticed your sign said this place was established in 1856."

"Yes Bill."

"Well I don't want to be rude, being as I am a guest and all, but I thought that Fripp Island really didn't start getting developed until the 1960's. I read somewhere that it was used as a hunting range up until that time when they built bridges connecting it to Beaufort."

"Well aren't you just smart as a whip. Where did you find this one?" She said smirking at Fripp.

"You are correct Bill. This settlement actually used to be a hunting lodge. Men would come up here and stay in the cottages to hunt or fish. They had to get here by boat. The main house is actually fairly new, built within the last 15 years."

"So why the 1856 then?"

She smiled, "Well, we put that for the tourists really. They all want to feel like they are a part of history. They want to feel like they are part of something bigger than themselves. So we give them what they want. But they wouldn't know the difference between 1856 and 1956. Most of them that is," she said winking at Bill.

"Hi Daddy!" A voice announced as the screen door opened.

"Bill, meet my daughter Sienna."

All heads turned toward the door. Bill was taken aback by Sienna's beauty. She looked like a young Sophia Loren. Obviously Sienna got her good looks from her mother.

"Hi. I'm Bill, pleased to meet you."

Sienna had just come in from swimming in the ocean. She was still in her bikini and was putting her long auburn hair up into a pony tail. Bill tried to fight the urge to stare out of respect for Fripp, but Sienna's hazel-green eyes were captivating. Fripp cleared his throat to get Bill's attention.

"How come you're here at the inn, Daddy?" Sienna asked as she walked over and gave Fripp a hug and a kiss.

"I brought Bill out here to stay for a couple of days while I attend to some business in Charleston. Then I will be back to get him."

"Why doesn't he just stay at the hotel?"

"He likes things a little quieter. He is a student of history," Fripp offered.

"Well Bill, it's quiet around here almost to the point of being boring," Sienna stated discouragingly, while staring at her mother and emphasizing the word boring. "Maybe you will liven things up," she toyed, sending her glance towards Bill.

Now Bill liked this place even more.

Louanne had been preparing lunch prior to the interruption. "Lunch is almost ready if you'd all like to come and sit down," she said, motioning to the picnic table out front. When she brought the food out and everyone had been served, everyone dug in but Bill. He lowered his head to pray, leaving the other three looking around confused, and sending Sienna into a quiet fit of giggles.

"This is delicious Louanne. Thank you," Bill expressed, once he had raised his head and taken his first bite.

"Thanks for the compliment Bill. You're different from other guests Fripp has brought us."

When lunch was finished, Fripp excused himself to head back to Charleston. Sienna went off to do some chores around the inn. Bill offered to do the dishes and help clean up the kitchen.

As evening was approaching, Louanne and Bill were sitting out in the screened-in porch. Sienna came out of the main cottage, "I'm heading down for a walk on the beach. Would you like to come along Bill?" she asked.

"Nah, I think I'll just hang out here. Thanks anyway."

"Okay, suit yourself," Sienna huffed, and stalked off.

When Sienna was out of earshot Louanne counseled, "Bill, you need to let go of her." Louanne spoke with a strong yet very feminine voice. The hint of her Irish accent was coming through giving authority to her words.

"Pardon?"

"When a beautiful young woman asks you to go for a walk on the beach and you decline, it has to be because you are hurting about another girl. You need to let go of whoever the girl is who you are brooding over. If it was meant to be, she would be here with you. I can tell that you are carrying a lot of pain."

"I guess it shows. I just can't help it."

"What do you want out of life, Bill?" Louanne prodded.

Bill paused to think, "Happiness, I suppose."

"And what is happiness?"

"I don't know."

"Young ladies don't know what affect their guiles have on young men. You will need time to get over this. It's a bad thing. Let me ask you, if something happened to you that seemed horrible and then takes you in a completely different path from what you wanted but then led you to something greater, was it really a bad thing that happened to you? Or was it a good thing?"

"You make a good point Louanne. I guess it would be a good thing."

"I heard a story once about two sisters in the concentration camp," Louanne continued. "Conditions were atrocious. To top it off, the bunkhouse they were in was infested with fleas. The sisters thought that it was more than they could take. Theirs was the only bunkhouse infested with fleas. Later, they found that the women in the other bunkhouses had been raped by the guards but the guards had left the women from their bunkhouse alone because of the fleas. So really, the flea infestation was a good thing."

"I hear what you're saying. It's just so painful right now."

"Leave the past behind son. Go for a walk on the beach. The waves have a calming effect."

Bill smiled at Louanne and nodded. He headed toward the beach to catch up with Sienna. Maybe Louanne was right, maybe this was just the distraction that he needed to move on and forget about Erica.

"So my company is good enough for you after all," Sienna coyly pointed out once Bill had found her. Sienna was almost eighteen. At times she bounced around and chatted like a young teenage girl. But she was every inch a woman. Her beauty was beyond compare. And she came off very intelligent and quite mature for her age.

Bill was feeling a little embarrassed and a little nervous. "I'm sorry," Bill offered. "It's nothing to do with you or your company." Now he was feeling bashful.

Sienna could sense Bill checking her out and flung her hair back over her shoulder to encourage him even more. Bill turned his head to look the other way. "Listen to the waves," Sienna said. "It's such a peaceful sound."

Sienna and Bill continued walking along the beach. Bill explained what had happened with Erica and how Fripp had given him a place to stay. He related the story that Jack had told him, explaining what Jack had done and the trouble that he was now in. Sienna listened as Bill told his story. They walked along the beach for over an hour then turned around to walk back to the inn.

"I have a baseball game tomorrow night in Beaufort," Sienna announced. "Would you like to come and watch? It might take your mind off things."

"Well I don't care much for baseball but I think that I would like to go to your game."

"You don't much care for baseball! What kind of American are you?"

"Well actually, I'm from Canada."

"I thought so with that accent of yours."

"Accent? What accent?" Bill protested.

"Never mind. Whereabouts in Canada?"

"It's a little place called Grand Valley—near Toronto."

"Well okay Valley Boy, tomorrow night you are going to get a taste of good old American baseball."

About one hundred people sat in the stands watching the Beaufort BBQ Queens team play against the Bluffton Belles. Sienna was sitting on the bench for the first part of the game. She was the alternate pitcher and the coach decided to go with the first string pitcher for tonight's game. Because she wasn't in the game yet, Sienna came up to the stands to sit with Bill a few times and explain to him how the scoring went and a little about each of the players on her team. Sienna would sit so that her thigh was touching Bill's thigh and her shoulder was against his. She would lean her face in when she talked to him and he could smell the sweet scent of her hair.

Whenever Sienna would go up into the stands some of the girls on her team would look back over their shoulders curiously. Some even made some heckling comments toward them. All was in fun of course.

Part way through the game, the Bluffton Belles had the bases loaded on Sienna's team. There were no players out yet. The pitcher on Sienna's team came over to the bench at a time-out and told the coach to put Sienna in. The coach didn't want to but other players on the Beaufort team started to encourage him that Sienna could do it and he should put her in. Reluctantly the coach agreed.

Bill didn't know a lot about baseball but he knew enough that this was a desperate situation calling for strong nerves and skill. Sienna got to have a couple of warm-up pitches and then the ump called, "Play ball!"

Sienna threw her first pitch, "Steerikke!" The next pitch and the next pitch were the same. When the umpire announced, "You're owwwt!" Sienna's team started cheering and whistling enthusiastically.

The second batter came to the plate and hit Sienna's first pitch. Bill's heart was in his throat. He was really pulling for his new friend. The ump called the ball fowl. Sienna then threw three strikes to take the second batter out. Again, Sienna's team cheered and whistled along with most of the crowd.

As the third batter, approached home plate, the crowd grew silent. Could she handle this stress and not choke, Bill wondered, along with everyone else. Could she strike out three batters in a row under this kind of pressure?

Sienna threw her first pitch—a perfect strike.

Sienna threw her second pitch—another strike.

The crowd was so quiet now that Bill could hear his heart beating. Sienna glanced up to where he was sitting and smiled at him. She threw her pitch. "Steerikke!" The crowd jumped to their feet and cheered. Sienna's team rushed out to congratulate her. The game wasn't over yet but the rest of the action paled in comparison to these last few minutes.

After the game, Bill came down from the stands and told Sienna that he was impressed and that she did great. Sienna was on cloud nine. She had just played a great ball game and some of her teammates thought that she had a new beau—a handsome one at that.

Bill and Sienna drove over to the BBQ Queen to grab a hamburger and milkshake. They met up with some of Sienna's team-mates who continued their heckling. "*Sienna and Bill sitting in a tree k-i-s-s-i-n-g.*

First comes love. Then comes marriage. Then comes Sienna with the baby carriage."

Bill and Sienna laughed this off but each in their hearts felt a little bit of wishful thinking that maybe that scenario would play out.

"A bunch of us are going down to the beach to have a campfire," Karen, the back-catcher told Sienna. "If you and your fella want to come y'all are welcome."

Sienna looked at Bill with a questioning glance and Bill acknowledged with a nod, "Sure, why not." Sienna smiled, in part because she wanted to go to the campfire and in part because the other girls were thinking that Bill and her were together.

Most of Sienna's teammates and their boyfriends were at the campfire when Sienna and Bill arrived. As she approached the fire, the team cheered for Sienna once again in acknowledgment of her accomplishment at the game. Bill smiled at her. They sat down by the fire near Karen and her boyfriend, who was playing the guitar.

It was still warm out so the campfire was less for heat and more as a gathering place. Flames and sparks ascended upwards toward the clear starry sky. It was getting warm sitting by the fire.

"Do you want to take a walk down by the water?" Sienna whispered into Bill's ear.

"Yeah," Bill responded as he got up and then reached down with his hand to assist Sienna getting up from the sand. Sienna took Bill's hand but did not let go after she was on her feet. She continued to hold his hand and put her other hand on his bicep as they walked toward the ocean.

When they reached the water's edge, Sienna turned to Bill and kissed him on his cheek. "Thank you for coming to my game tonight." They stood there for a moment looking into each other's eyes and then slowly moved towards each other's lips. Sienna and Bill engaged in a long, passionate kiss, that Bill would later describe as life altering.

Louanne let Bill stay in cabin number 3 in exchange for doing some chores around the inn. It was the smallest of the cabins, room for just one. She said it was usually the hippie loner types who occupied it. They were either hitchhiking their way across country, or trying to write the great American novel, or trying to find themselves and define their lives by nature. She said they rented it to some writer once, she couldn't remember his name, who went on to have his novel published. She had a copy of it somewhere, signed by him and a note thanking them for his stay.

Bill put his few belongings away in the small two-drawer chest beside his twin bed. It wasn`t much to look at, but he guessed looks didn't matter inside when you're this close to the great outdoors. A twin bed in one corner, a small writing desk and chair in the other, it was all you really needed. Louanne said she would bring him out fresh linens before the night. He grabbed the pad of Blue Dolphin Inn stationary from the desk and a pen and went out to the porch and took a much needed seat in the rocking chair.

Bill began to sketch. But it wasn`t the water or the trees that inspired him, no, it was Sienna. And as he sat there sketching her, he thought to himself that maybe it wasn`t so bad that he was seeing all this without Erica. Maybe it was like Louanne had said, that it had happened for the better.

Sienna came bopping up carrying a basket with linens. "Ma sent me out to give these to you. What'cha drawing?"

He quickly flipped the paper over. "Nothing, just the view. Beautiful view," he said.

"It is. But I'd much rather be in the city with my dad, there's so much more adventure and excitement."

"Do you ever go and stay there?"

"A few times a year mom lets me go. Mostly in winter when things are basically dead here and she doesn't need my help. But she refuses to go. She hasn`t been to the city with my dad since she brought me home. She says she was born a country girl and she'll stay one. She hates the busyness of the city and she especially hates the Tavern. She says I'll be corrupted if I go there too often. But what she doesn't know is that I think I've got more of a chance being corrupted here," she laughed. "All the teens here are so bored they are actively looking for things to get themselves into trouble with."

"But not you right?" Bill said with a smirk.

"Of course not me," Sienna said slyly back.

"So what do you all do for fun around here then?" he asked.

"Oh don't get me wrong, there's lots of fun stuff to do. It's not as bad as I make it out to be. We go canoeing and have bonfires and some weekends there are parties at the rec centre in town. It's just not as exciting as the city."

"Trust me, the city isn't all that great. You've got a good thing here, nice and quiet."

"Oh, you're one of *those*," she teased.

"One of what?" he retorted.

"An old fogy!"

They burst out laughing.

Each evening after supper and when they had finished their chores, Bill and Sienna would take a walk along the beach. Bill was really starting to find that it was just as Louanne had said—the waves had a calming effect.

"So Bill," Sienna started to probe as they walked along the beach, "you haven't told me about your parents yet."

"There isn't really a lot to tell. They were good parents. I have two brothers and four sisters. My parents worked hard and raised us right. They both made many sacrifices. There was a lot of love in our house when we were growing up."

"What did they think of you coming down to Charleston for the summer?"

"My mom was okay with it. My dad isn't around anymore."

"Oh, I'm sorry to hear that," Sienna empathized. "How did he die?"

"It was an accident. I was with him."

Sienna could sense sadness in Bill's voice, "Do you want to talk about it?"

"We were on a canoe trip in Algonquin Park with a group from an outdoors club. It was really late in the season to do a trip but we loved canoeing and were trying to get one last trip in. It was pretty cold out. As we drove into the park, there was ice on the puddles. The club leader had warned us that if we fell into the water we would probably suffer hypothermia within two minutes. My dad and I had the smallest canoe and we had quite a bit of weight in our packs so we didn't have a lot of clearance from the water. We had made our way through a few lakes and portages and then we came to a very large lake. The rest of the canoes hugged the shoreline, but my dad and I went right across the middle of the lake. The wind picked up quite a bit and we noticed that the rest of the group pulled into the shore. Thinking that they had decided to set up camp, we turned towards the shore. After paddling very hard to get to them, we called out asking if they were setting up camp. They yelled back that they had pulled in because they were all taking on water. I guess this was because the waves were higher along the shoreline. They told us if we weren't taking on water to just keep going. It was so cold that we had icicles forming on the gunnels of the canoe.

"I was in the stern and my dad was in the bow. We turned the canoe back out towards the middle of the lake but had to go around a point. As we rounded the point a wave hit us broadside. I tried to steer the canoe so that we were cutting through the waves but a second wave hit us right after the first. I was kneeling down and the water was already up to my thighs. Another wave hit us and the stern went under water while the bow went up in the air. My dad was still paddling, not realizing that we were going down. I went under and then the canoe rolled over on both of us.

"The water was freezing. It was so cold that it took my breath away. They always say that if you capsize, you should stay with your boat. We both hung onto the canoe for a few minutes. I could no longer feel my fingers. I told my dad that I was going to try and swim to shore. Letting go of the canoe, I floated on my back and then kicked my feet even though I was wearing hiking boots. I made it to shore but this section of the shoreline was a straight up twenty-five foot cliff. At about knee deep below the water's surface, I found a ledge that I could stand on, and then I grabbed branches that were sticking out of the rocks and pulled myself up the cliff. When I reached the top, I turned to look at the canoe and didn't see my dad. My heart sunk.

"Then I heard him calling from further down the shore. After making my way through the woods to the spot that he was at, I grabbed branches and lowered myself back down to the waterline so that my dad could grab my pant-leg and pull himself out of the water. We made our way back up to the top of the cliff. Then turning around, we could see our packs, paddles, and overturned canoe floating away. Standing there on the cliff, the bitter wind was cutting right through our wet clothes.

"A few minutes later, the rest of the group rounded the point. I can only imagine the shock they felt when they saw our gear floating but didn't see us. We started to call out to them. It only took about twenty minutes for them to get to shore and get a fire started for us. I was so frozen that I couldn't undress myself to put some dry clothes on. A couple of the other guys had to do that for me.

"That night, we kept the fire going and a bunch of us slept right beside the fire, in our sleeping bags, with legs overlapping each other to keep warm. As I lay there, looking up at the sky, it started to snow. I could feel the snowflakes landing on my face and melting. This was quite a shock to our systems. Being young, my body could handle it. My dad wasn't so fortunate. Sometime during the night, he passed away. Earlier in the evening, he had been telling people how proud he was of me that I saved his life." Bill's eyes started to water.

"Oh Bill, that must have been a horrible experience." Sienna and Bill continued walking hand in hand along the beach.

Near the end of June, a group of young women had booked one of the cabins for a weekend long bachelorette party. Louanne was sitting on the front porch of the main inn watching the ladies cavorting around in front of their cabin. They were drinking and sunbathing and of course watching Bill go about doing his chores. Louanne could tell that they were eyeing him up.

Walking over to where Bill was working she reasoned, "You know Bill, there are two questions that if your girlfriend or wife asks you it's in your best interest to never answer. The first is, when referring to another female, 'Do you think she is pretty?' No matter what answer you give, you can't win. If you say no, then your girl will not believe you or think you don't have very good taste. If you say yes, then you are going to be in trouble for noticing."

"So what does a fellow do Louanne?"

"Just avoid giving an answer," Louanne reasoned as she started to saunter away.

"Wait a minute Louanne. What was the second question?" Bill pleaded.

"That one, my son, you will have to find out for yourself."

Soon thereafter, Sienna appeared with a cold glass of lemonade for Bill, "Sooo, those girls seem to be paying a lot of attention to you Bill. Do you think they're pretty?"

"I hadn't really noticed Sienna, I was so busy doing my work and thinking about you and me taking a walk on the beach later and stopping at our favorite kissing spot."

Sienna kissed Bill on the cheek and then with a spring in her step headed back toward the main inn. Bill could see Louanne sitting on the front porch. When their eyes met, she smiled and nodded at him. Bill smiled back. Louanne had just given him excellent advice. But what was the other question?

BEAUFORT

JUNE & JULY 1976

1 976 was the year of the American bi-centennial. Most of America was celebrating and Beaufort was no different than any other small American town. Sienna worked part-time at the BBQ Queen, one of the local hamburger shops in Beaufort and also the sponsor of Sienna's baseball team. Bill usually had his chores completed by mid-morning so he took the opportunity to catch a ride into town with Sienna and hang out while she was doing her shift at work. He figured he could spend some time researching history and give a little thought to how he could get his hands on that treasure.

Sometimes Bill would grab some research material and spend his day sitting in the park at the foot of Bay Street at Carteret Street. Bill noticed the comings and goings of people. Two people who really intrigued Bill were T. W. Wolfe and Nathaniel Brown.

Bill's first encounter with T.W. Wolfe was on a beautiful summer morning. Sienna had dropped Bill off in downtown Beaufort with arrangements to pick him up after work. Bill grabbed a coffee to go at a café next to Luther's Pharmacy on Bay Street then walked down to the waterfront. He took a seat on a park bench and sipped on his coffee. It was cool enough to drink by then. The smell of the ocean waffling down the Beaufort River from Port Royal, the sound of the sea gulls, and the warmth of the coffee gave Bill a pleasant satisfied feeling of well-being. His troubles seemed a million miles away. He closed his eyes for a moment and turned his face toward the sun. He was thinking about Sienna, her beauty, her lips, the smell of her, her smile, her carefree way. This was good. Suddenly, Bill's moment of total transcendence was interrupted by a rustling sound nearby.

From out of nowhere, Thaddeus Winston Wolfe appeared. Wolfe was a man in his seventies. He had white hair and a long white beard. Both were shaggy and dirty. Although the temperature was already about eighty degrees, T.W. was wearing a knee length winter parka, black rubber boots, a woolen toque, and winter gloves with the thumbs and fingers worn through. Wrapped around his neck was a long scarf. Wolfe sauntered through the waterfront park. As he walked, his parka would open revealing that he was wearing pajamas under his odd outer garb. These too were worn, torn, and dirty.

Wolfe looked at Bill looking at him. Wolfe half grunted, half growled at Bill who then looked away embarrassed. Wolfe rambled over to a garbage can and started rummaging through it. He would select some items to put in the pockets of his parka. Occasionally, Wolfe would come across some food that he would eat. Sometimes, the food was obviously rotten as Wolfe would spit it out on the ground in disgust. The sea gulls swarmed around him, hoping to get something to eat and he flung his arms at them like a mad man. It was a very bewildering scene. Periodically, Wolfe would stop and glare over at Bill who would then look away immediately.

Wolfe moved on to the next garbage can and repeated his routine. As Wolfe drew closer to the bench where Bill was sitting, Bill became a little uncomfortable. He didn't know whether Wolfe was going to hurt him or just pass by. Bill, deducing that Wolfe was homeless, did feel a bit sorry for him so he reached into his pocket drawing out some money to offer him for food.

"Keep your money son," a soft, yet raspy, female voice came from behind. "He won't take your money and he don't need your money. That there is T.W. Wolfe. His daddy was one of the richest men in the Lowcountry."

Bill turned to see a woman approaching. She was about in her mid-thirties.

"Sadie's the name." She sat down on the bench uncomfortably close to Bill for his liking. Sadie carried a knitting bag and when she sat it on the bench it made such a loud thud that Bill knew it didn't contain any knitting. He suspected that there was some form of alcoholic beverage inside based on the thud and the fact that Sadie smelled like a distillery when she spoke. "Yup, it's sad," Sadie continued, "old T.W. was left all his daddy's money, lives in one of the biggest houses in town, and is crazier than a bag of hammers."

"Why is he like that?" Bill asked.

"Oh he wasn't always like that. T.W. used to run his daddy's business for him when T.W. was in his late teens and early twenties. He was a good looking young man. Had all the ladies after him too. Then all of a sudden one day he just started acting crazy. Nobody knows why. His poor daddy tried every which way he could to get T.W. help." Sadie reached into her knitting bag and pulled out a bottle of Jack Daniels. She took a swig from the bottle then offered the bottle to Bill. Bill declined by waving his hand and holding up his coffee to show that he already had something to drink. "Drove his daddy to an early death so he did," Sadie concluded.

"What about his mother?" Bill asked, his interest now piqued.

"She done run off when T.W. started acting crazy. She couldn't stand the embarrassment, her being a society lady and all."

Bill and Sadie sat on the bench watching T.W. Wolfe continue from garbage can to garbage can then walk toward Bay Street and disappear among the buildings. Sadie continued sipping on her Jack Daniels throughout the morning. Bill watched the comings and goings of people along the waterfront. There were a couple of small boats in the harbor that provided some visual entertainment for Bill.

"Some say it was a woman," Sadie broke the silence.

"Pardon?"

"Some say it was a woman that made T.W. start acting crazy."

"Oh," Bill was no longer thinking about T.W. Wolfe. Bill's thoughts were focused on his own situation. However, since Sadie had broken the silence, he thought he would take the opportunity to address something that he had been wondering about. Sadie was dressed in period costume from the antebellum era complete with bonnet and all. Beaufort had several events happening over the summer with characters dressed in period costumes. "So Sadie," Bill started, "which character are you playing?"

"What are you talking about?"

"Aren't you in one of the plays or skits the Chamber of Commerce is putting on?"

"No. I'm not," Sadie answered. "Why do you ask?"

"No reason," Bill hesitated, "It's just that I thought almost everyone in town was taking part in those plays."

"Not me."

Bill leaned his head back so that his face was pointing directly at the sun, taking in its entire splendor. He closed his eyes. T.W. Wolfe isn't the only crazy one around here, he thought.

"H . . . H . . . Have y . . . y . . . y . . . y'all g . . . g . . . got any yard work needs doin'?" Bill opened his eyes to see in front of him another strange looking man. "H . . . H . . . Have y . . . y . . . y . . . y'all g . . . g . . . got any yard work needs doin'?" the man repeated.

"No, I don't have a yard."

"Th . . . Th . . . Th . . . This yard needs some work. Isn't th . . . th . . . th . . . this y . . . y . . . your yard?"

"No, it's not mine," Bill said defensively.

Bill looked at Sadie with a quizzical look.

"Go ahead Nathaniel. Tidy this yard," Sadie directed.

"G . . . G . . . Goody!" Nathaniel responded gleefully. "Th . . . That'll be one dollar for all this work. P . . . P . . . Payable in advance. I don't want to get ripped off ya know."

"Pay the man Bill for cleaning up your yard," Sadie snickered.

Bill pulled out one dollar from his pocket and handed it to Nathaniel.

"Where d . . . d . . . d . . . do you want me to start mister?"

"How about over by the water's edge?"

"Okay."

As Nathaniel walked over to the water's edge Sadie spoke up, "Nathaniel Brown. His parents are rich too. Filthy rich."

"Is everybody around here with rich parents crazy?" Bill asked rhetorically. "I'm glad I'm not rich nor my parents."

Nathaniel Brown, Sadie & T.W. Wolfe, Beaufort South Carolina 1976

Nathaniel was a slim man about the same age as Bill. He wore very thick glasses. Nathaniel was dressed in a very neatly pressed dress shirt with a bow-tie. He had on dress shorts, knee socks, and highly polished dress shoes. This was hardly the attire to wear for yard work. Nathaniel rode a bicycle that he had rigged up to transport gardening tools, rakes, and shovels. There was a large carrier on the front of the bicycle and another on the back.

As it drew toward noon, Bill stood up, stretched, and nodded to Sadie, "I'm heading to the library. I'm doing some research on local history. See you around eh?"

"Eh? So y'all are from Canada."

"Well I am," Bill chuckled to himself as he continued walking toward Bay Street, leaving Sadie stone faced, confused by his joke.

About mid afternoon, Sienna met Bill downtown and they headed back toward Fripp Island. Bill related to Sienna about the strange characters that he had interacted with that day. Sienna knew who Bill was talking about since she had seen them around town before. Even though she'd lived in the area all her life she'd never had any such interactions with them.

"Bill," Sienna shyly interjected, "our baseball team is sponsoring a dance-a-thon to raise money for a local charity. It's a week this Friday and goes for twenty-four hours. The guy who was going to be my partner just cancelled. Would you maybe go in it with me? Just as friends of course."

Even though they had shared a passionate kiss at the campfire on the beach, Bill still felt connected to Erica and Sienna had easily picked up on that. At the same time he was starting to have real feelings for Sienna. He couldn't stop thinking about her. But he also thought about Erica and couldn't quite get over his heartbreak yet.

"Sure, why not. It sounds like fun. But I've never danced that long in my life."

"Me either."

Sienna was happy that Bill accepted her invitation. She was starting to become very fond of him. When they arrived back at The Blue Dolphin Inn, Louanne had supper all prepared. "Fripp came by here this morning with some papers and books for you to look at Bill. They are over in the corner in that old saddle bag."

"Thanks Louanne. Did he say what I'm to do with them?"

"He said that you will have to look through them all and figure out where the treasure is hidden. Ha! Oh that man. What a kidder. Treasure! Ha!"

Two days later, Sienna had to work another shift so Bill hitched a ride into Beaufort with her so that he could do some more research at the library. The library wasn't open until early afternoon so Bill had Sienna drop him off downtown. He grabbed a coffee and went to sit by the waterfront. Bill brought the saddle bag with him.

"Morning Sadie," Bill chirped as he took a seat on the bench.

"Morning son."

T.W. Wolfe was already making his rounds along the waterfront. When his eye caught Bill's, he growled. Bill wasn't bothered by him now. He just pulled some of the documents from the saddle bag and began to study them.

"What's that y'all are working on," Sadie asked.

"It's a little history project. I'm trying to find some lost treasure," Bill didn't mind telling Sadie because he felt that either she wouldn't believe him or if she did and told others, they wouldn't believe her.

"Hear that T.W.? The kid here is looking for treasure." T.W. Wolfe stopped picking through his current garbage can project and looked over at Sadie and Bill. He then grunted and started picking through the garbage can again.

Before long Nathaniel Brown showed up. "C . . . C . . . C . . . Can I tidy your yard again today mister?"

"Sure Nate. Start down by the water's edge again. You did a great job before. Is it still one dollar?"

"Y . . . Y . . . Yes sir. One d . . . d . . . dollar in advance because I don't want . . ."

" . . . To get ripped off. I know Nate. Here's your dollar."

"Th . . . Th . . . Thanks mister and it's N . . . N . . . N . . . Nathaniel—not Nate."

And so this was the start of a regular routine, Nathaniel Brown tidying Bill's yard on a daily basis—even though the property actually belonged to the Town of Beaufort.

T.W. Wolfe watched Bill and Nathaniel Brown interact. He watched Bill sitting on the bench chatting with Sadie. As this happened time after time, T.W. seemed to feel more and more comfortable with Bill being in the park. T.W. started to approach closer to Bill as he passed by on his way out of the park toward Bay Street. One day, T.W. came right over to the bench and growled, "Treasure, humph."

Bill, trying not to let T.W. get to him, whispered to himself a scripture that his mother had drilled into him as a child, "As far as it depends on you, be peaceable with all men."

Nathaniel Brown must have been within earshot because he started to sing, "As far as it depends on you be peaceable with all men, as far as it depends on you be peaceable with all men." Nathaniel actually had a very good singing voice and he didn't stutter when he was singing.

One day when they were doing their regular one dollar transaction, Bill asked Nathaniel to sing the words, *As far as.* Nathaniel did this without stuttering. Bill had Nathaniel repeat it several times and then got Nathaniel to say it—not sing it. Nathaniel did this perfectly. Bill explained, "Now that you are comfortable saying that Nathaniel, any time that you feel you might stutter, just start your sentence with 'as far as'." From that time on, Nathaniel started a lot of sentences with 'as far as' and Bill started to call Nathaniel by the nickname 'As Far As.' Nathaniel liked it and the two men quickly formed a special bond.

The Friday night of the dance-a-thon arrived. It was to start at six o'clock p.m. and go until Saturday night at six o'clock. Sienna and Bill arrived about five thirty and Sienna took Bill around and introduced him again to her friends on her baseball team. Most of the girls on Sienna's baseball team were sixteen or seventeen years old. So when seventeen year-old Sienna showed up with the twenty year-old boy who had come to watch her ball game, and then shown up with her at the beach camp fire, her friends gave her a nudge-nudge, wink-wink signal of approval.

Sienna and Bill were having fun dancing to the fast music. When the disc-jockey slowed things down, they shyly moved toward each other and wrapped their arms around each other. Bill and Sienna were able to talk as they danced in each other's arms. Every hour they were allowed a five-minute break to grab a drink, something to eat, or use the bathroom.

"You two look like you are getting pretty close," Karen, the back-catcher from the ball team, commented to Sienna in the bathroom.

"Yeah," Beth, the short-stop cut in. "You better be careful or you will find that you are soon getting married."

"That wouldn't be so bad," Sienna responded.

"Yeah, he is cute," Karen acknowledged.

"Sienna, you better hang onto him or half the girls on our team will be after him," Beth warned.

"Oh, I plan to hang onto him. So just stay away you two. I think I am in love."

The music started again signaling the dancers to come back to the floor. The disc-jockey started the set with Rick Dees' "Disco Duck" which got everybody moving and laughing. After a few fast songs, the DJ played Rod Stewart's "Tonight's the Night." Sienna moved in close to Bill and snuggled her head into his chest.

"Rod Stewart is one of my favorites," she whispered.

"Now, he'll be one of mine," Bill responded softly, enjoying the closeness. "I really like Loggins and Messina," Bill continued the conversation.

"They are good. Too bad they are talking about breaking up," Sienna added.

"I noticed that Sunday night at the theatre, 'Rocky' is playing. Would you like to go?"

"I would rather go to Savannah and see 'All the President's Men'."

"Sure. As friends?" Bill asked, hoping for a different response.

"Well, how about as a date?"

"Even better," Bill smiled.

By the time six o'clock on Saturday night had rolled around, Sienna and Bill had talked about every subject that they possibly could. They had danced the fast dances together, laughed together, and pressed their bodies together during the slow dances. By six o'clock, they were a couple.

Louanne came to pick Sienna and Bill up to drive them back to the Blue Dolphin Inn as she figured that they would be pretty tired—too tired to drive. Louanne arrived to catch the last hour of the dance-a-thon. On the drive back to the Inn, Sienna sat in the middle while Bill sat by the window of Louanne's pick-up truck. Bill soon fell asleep. "You and Bill are getting along quite well I see."

"I'm in love mom," Sienna whispered to her mother.

Tuesday morning following the dance-a-thon, Sienna had another shift at the BBQ Queen so Bill caught a ride in to Beaufort with her. Bill went through his usual routine of grabbing a coffee and heading down to the waterfront park to do some reading and research. He took his seat on the bench next to Sadie. T. W. Wolfe was already scrounging about the garbage cans and kept looking over at Bill as he slowly moved towards him. T. W. walked straight up to Bill and stopping in front of him blurted, "You've got to be carefully taught."

"Pardon," Bill asked as T.W. was already moving away from Bill and Sadie.

"That's the first time that I've heard T.W. talk in years," Sadie slurred.

"My grandfather used to say that to me all the time," Bill pondered out loud. "Wait a minute, T.W!" Bill shouted as he got up and started after him.

Noticing that Bill was coming after him, T.W. started moving faster toward the downtown area. "Sister Anne, Sister Anne, do you see anybody coming?" T.W. called out and was gone. T.W. had disappeared in behind Fordham's Hardware Store.

Bill stopped in his tracks. It was as if he had walked into a brick wall.

"What is it now?" Sadie asked.

"My grandfather used to tell me a story about some kids being held prisoner and in part of the story there was a line just like what T.W. said—Sister Anne, Sister Anne, do you see anybody coming?" What connection was there, Bill wondered, with T. W. and Bill's grandfather? The things that had happened to him and the people that he'd met since he arrived in Charleston were just too weird, too bizarre—except for Sienna, of course. Bill was feeling part jubilation and part fear that he was involved in some master plan that he was supposed to find this treasure.

Bill sat back down on the bench beside Sadie who took out her bottle from her knitting bag and took a long swig.

"Why do you drink so much Sadie?"

"I don't know," Sadie responded defensively.

"Sorry Sadie, that answer's not good enough."

"I guess it's because of the things I've done in my life. I don't really like myself."

"Do you want to talk about it?" Bill empathized.

"What are you, a shrink?"

"No Sadie, just a friend."

"I was in a play in high school and this boy that I liked and I did it behind the stage. I got pregnant and my parents made me give the baby up for adoption."

"That's not so bad Sadie."

"Easy for you to say. It haunts me to this day, constantly wondering what has happened to that little baby girl—what has become of her? She would be seventeen now, almost eighteen."

"Sadie, did you know that in the Bible, Paul had gone around persecuting Christians and having them put to death. Yet, Jesus picked him as an Apostle. God forgave him. Jehovah God sent his son Jesus to earth to die for us so that we could have our sins forgiven."

"Now you sound like a preacher!"

"Again Sadie, I'm just a friend who cares. If God can forgive Paul for what he did, surely he forgives you for what you've done and who are you to say no to God's forgiveness?"

"When you put it that way, I have to forgive myself. But I've been drinking so long it would be hard to stop."

"Just take it a little bit at a time Sadie, a little bit at a time. No matter how much you drink Sadie, you can't change what's in the past."

"You seem too wise for your age son."

"Not really Sadie. Just experienced. My father was an alcoholic and I learned the Bible from my mother."

On Wednesday, Sienna didn't have a shift at work but Bill wanted to go back to Beaufort to see if he could talk to T. W. Wolfe. Sitting in the park beside Sadie, Bill could see T.W. a little ways away. Bill called out the next line in his grandfather's story, that followed the line 'Sister Anne, Sister Anne, do you see anybody coming,' "no but the cock's crowin' and the wind's blowin' and there's three men on horseback far, far away."

T. W. stopped and looked up at Bill with a grin. T.W. walked over to the bench and sat down beside Sadie. Sadie promptly moved over, in part because she was uncomfortable with T.W.'s uncharacteristic actions and in part because of his unpleasant body odor. Bill sat on the ground in front of the bench facing T.W. and Sadie.

"Do you have the pocket watch?"

Bill was not sure what T.W. was talking about. He did have a pocket watch that was given to him by his grandfather and was told that it had been in the family for a long, long time. Bill reached into his pocket and taking out the pocket watch held it up in front of T.W. T.W.'s eyes lit up and his filthy hands reached out and took the tarnished watch. As he turned the watch over and over examining it he read some initials on it, "RKD." "Robert Keith Dick," he surmised.

Bill remembered the name Robert Keith Dick from the story that Jack Falstaff had told him. But how did T.W. Wolfe know about these things and was he crazy or wasn't he?

"You've got to be carefully taught!" T.W. read the inscription on the watch aloud. "You've got to be carefully taught." He read again. Then he stood up and started dancing around with the watch as his partner, singing, "You've got to be carefully taught. You've got to be carefully taught. You've got to be carefully taught." T.W. was waving his arms in the air and jumping up and down in ecstasy. Then he turned and bolted right for the water. He ran out until the water reached waist height on him and then dunked himself under. Coming back up to the surface, T.W. ran back to Bill and Sadie who were dumbfounded. T.W. placed the watch in Bill's hand carefully placing one of his hands underneath Bill's and the other over top in a gesture to ensure that the watch stayed put.

"What is going on?" Sadie asked, as it was still early enough in the day that she wasn't totally inebriated yet. It was as if the sight of the watch and dousing himself in the salt water actually brought a bit of sanity to T.W.

"You've got to be carefully taught!" T.W. exclaimed loudly to Sadie who still wasn't getting it. "You get taught at College! The treasure is at The College of Charleston!" T.W. continued excitedly while he opened Bill's hand and pointed to an inscription on the inside casing of the watch. *"Knowledge and wisdom are treasures and must be drawn up as waters from a cistern. You've got to be carefully taught."* RKD

"What treasure are you talking about?" Sadie asked.

"The treasure that he's looking for," T.W. explained nodding towards Bill. "I heard rumors about this treasure when I was in College."

"So you think there really might be a treasure?" Bill asked T.W.

"There is only one way to find out," T.W. stated.

That afternoon, when Bill returned to the Blue Dolphin Inn, Fripp and Jack Falstaff were waiting there for him. "Bill, I think that Jack and I have determined where the treasure might be. We think that it could be at 35 Meeting Street. You see 35 Meeting Street was built by William Bull Sr. in 1720."

"So," Jack broke in, "it was in existence when your ancestor would have sent the treasure over from Scotland."

"Not only that," Fripp grew excited. "William Bull Jr. was a doctor. There could be some tie between him and William Pasteur who was also a doctor."

Bill didn't tell about the event that day with T.W. Wolfe who thought that the treasure was at the College of Charleston. "Well," Bill offered, "we can't just go and ask people if we can search through their house to look for treasure."

"But it does make sense that it could be there Bill. You yourself said that it was probably somewhere right in sight of 37 Meeting Street."

"And with all the legends about 37 Meeting Street," Jack piped in, "there must be some truth to treasure being in that area."

"There is only one way to find out," Fripp surmised.

Bill was wondering what he should do and who he could trust. He really didn't have a good feeling about Jack, yet he was in love with Fripp's daughter Sienna, and Fripp and Jack seemed to be working on this together. On the other hand, Sadie and T.W. Wolfe were crazy. He wrestled with the decision of whether or not he should tell Fripp and Jack what he had heard. Either way, Bill decided, he needed them.

"I met this guy in Beaufort who knows about the treasure," Bill shared. "He seems to think that the treasure is at the College of Charleston."

35 Meeting Street

Charleston

July 1976

Thirty-five Meeting Street was built in 1720 by William Bull Senior. He also had a hand in establishing the College of Charleston. While it was true that William Bull Jr. received a medical degree, the history books did not tie him or his father to Dr. Alexander Dick of Scotland.

Bill returned to Charleston with Fripp and Jack Falstaff. He spent a few days wandering up and down Meeting Street and walking over to the College of Charleston trying to think of where the treasure could be and how he could get his hands on it. But that wasn't the only thing mystifying him.

Bill was intrigued by Thaddeus. People just don't go mad, he thought, there has to be a driving force, some reason, something that pushed him over the edge. While at the College of Charleston one afternoon, he visited the campus library. Leafing through old yearbooks he searched for the face of this mad man in his youth. His eyes almost passed over the black and white photo of the clean cut, twenty-something man grinning a full toothed smile. He looked happy, he looked normal. Bill even found T.W. in group pictures for the Track Team, Drama Club, and cast photos for the school's production that year of "Hamlet, Prince of Denmark". He was the picture of health and vitality, heck—he was the picture of normalcy. Sure pictures can lie, smiles can be misleading, but seeing the life that Thaddeus had and had no more, left Bill feeling unsettled. He felt a deep pain for T.W. and all that he had lost. Money was nothing if you didn't have your marbles. All the things he could have done with his life, all that he could have become. A review for the play stated:

"Thaddeus Wolfe stole the show as the young Prince of Denmark . . ."

The review went on to praise him and there was a brief interview included in which T.W. said he had dreams of making it in show business after college. The review closed by saying:

"Thaddeus Wolfe is a name not to forget. We may be seeing it one day up in lights, or on the playbill for a Broadway show."

He left the library with more questions than answers. The review filled his head—T.W. had "star power, and potential for greatness". Bill had to know what had happened to him. When he went back to Beaufort he would confront him and find out for good.

For now, he had more important things to focus on. As he paced up and down Meeting Street, he mulled over the only two clues that his ancestors had left him: *You've got to be carefully taught* and *Sister Anne, Sister Anne, do you see anybody coming? No but the wind's blowin' and the cock's crowin' and there's three men on horseback far, far away.*

Bill decided that the more likely of the two sites where treasure would be hidden was 35 Meeting Street. An impressive garden wall surrounded the yard at 35 Meeting Street, a three story house. Bill noticed a dormer window off the attic facing to the east. He thought to himself, could that be where the story about Sister Anne took place? Were the children held captive in that attic?

"You hoo! You hoo! Young man!" a voice called from the door.

Bill looked toward the front entry door to see a stately looking sultry, southern belle descending the steps. "Young man, I've noticed that y'all have been looking at my house for the past hour. Is there something the matter? Or is there something that I can help you with?"

"I'm sorry ma'am, I was doing some research for a documentary about the American Revolution and I was told that your home was in existence at that time. I was hoping that I might shoot some film inside and outside—with your permission of course."

"Well Randolph and I are very proud of our home. You are correct; our house was built prior to the American Revolution. It was built by William Bull Senior. There is a lot of history that is tied to our house. I will ask Randolph tonight. You may call back here tomorrow and I will let you know. My name is Beulah, Beulah Cooper and what is your name young man?"

"Oh, I'm, my name is, ah, I'm Zach, Zachary Owens. Sorry, I don't have my business cards with me. I will get you one for the next time I come. Thank you very much Mrs. Cooper."

"Oh we're such a nice polite young man aren't we? You can call me Beulah."

"Thank you Beulah."

Fripp and BS Jack could hardly believe it when Bill told them about his encounter with Beulah Cooper. Fripp used his connections to get Bill some business cards that read: "*Zach Owens—Historical Film Productions.*" Bill returned to 35 Meeting Street the following day and got a positive answer from Beulah Cooper. He had arranged to come back in two days time with his film crew. BS Jack was to arrange for all of the equipment.

Bill needed to round out his crew, and he had just the people in mind. He borrowed Fripp's car and headed to Beaufort the next morning. He found Sadie sitting at her usual spot and sat down next to her.

"Well, well," she said, "look who is back. Where'ya been?"

"Morning Sadie," he said, "I've been busy working on this project. Actually, that's why I'm here. I need your help."

"Oh," she said with a slight grin, trying to conceal her delight.

"You and Nathaniel, and T.W. too, are they around?"

"Haven't seen them yet, but you know they will be any time now. So what's this project Bill?"

Bill explained everything to Sadie, and the role he needed her to play.

"I get to be an actress! I've always wanted to be an actress." She said, no longer trying to hide her elation.

"Well you're going to be *pretending* to be an actress."

"Pretending, acting, it's all the same. I have to go prepare. This is the biggest thing that's ever happened to me!"

And she was gone just like that. Bill smiled to himself, taking enjoyment from her happiness. Just then Nathaniel came running along,

"Sa . . . Sa . . ." He paused, collected his thoughts and his breath, and started over. "As far as Sadie just told me I get to be a part of a something special!"

"That's right Nathaniel, you . . ." Bill said trailing off, as he saw T.W. coming. He handed Nathaniel a dollar.

"I'll tell you all about it soon. But can you clean up this yard first?"

He took the dollar and commenced with his usual work, a huge smile on his face. Bill called T.W. over and the man obliged, coming over and sitting at the end of the bench.

"I really want to let you in on hunting down this treasure, but I have to know some things. I have to know I can trust you. I have to know what happened to you. And I have to know how you know so much. You seem to know more about the clues to this treasure than I do, and it involves my ancestors."

There was a long pause. Then T.W. spoke.

"I'm not crazy." So began an honest and eye-opening conversation between the two men.

"When I attended the College of Charleston as a young man," T.W. started, "I had heard stories about hidden treasure at the College. I started to do research to try to find the treasure. My schoolmates thought that I was crazy. At that time, I was in love with a beautiful young woman who was friends with another girl who lived at 35 Meeting Street. We would go there to attend parties. While there one evening, I heard this girl's father tell a story about treasure from Scotland and how Robert Keith Dick and Anne Dick had stayed in the house. One day I was overcome with curiosity and decided to search for clues in the house. I made my way to the attic and found Robert Keith's journal. I had just started to read it when the girl's father came home. He thought that I was some sort of pervert stalking his daughter. I started to act crazy to save my girlfriend the embarrassment of her girlfriend's father's story. I've been carrying on this act ever since."

"So Sadie was right," Bill said. "It *was* on account of a woman."

"So," T.W. continued, "I had read enough to know that there was something to the stories and when I heard that you were looking for the treasure, I thought that I would somehow let you know that I knew about the clues."

"Why carry on the charade for so long?"

"It just took over my life. That and thinking about this treasure consumed me."

Bill thanked him for the truth then called Nathaniel over to explain his plan and what parts he needed them to play. And so, he had his crew.

"Good morning Beulah."

"Good morning Zach."

"I would like to introduce you to my crew. This is Jack, our cameraman, Fripp and Nathaniel our road crew, and these are our cast T.W. and Sadie."

"What is that awful odor?" Beulah asked while covering her nose and mouth.

"Oh, I'm sorry Beulah," Bill apologized. "T. W.'s costume is a little musty."

"A little musty, Zach, it is downright putrid," Beulah said in disgust. "Please don't have him in my house for very long."

"Well let's get started gang! Perhaps we could get a few outside shots. Beulah, would you mind showing Sadie and T.W. to the attic? I would like to get a shot from outside with Sadie standing at the window in the attic. Then I will come in and get some interior shots."

"Bill," Sadie whispered, "I think that woman is a little crazy. She keeps calling you Zach."

"That's okay Sadie. Don't worry about it."

Thirty-five Meeting Street was a wonderful example of Charleston architecture at the time of the American Revolution. Mr. and Mrs. Cooper had maintained the historical architectural features inside and out while still updating and modernizing the facilities. The Coopers had collected antiques and artifacts from the Revolutionary era to furnish the home. Entering the home was like stepping into the past.

Upstairs in the attic, Sadie went over to the arched window and waved to Jack who had the camera set up to shoot the film. T.W. started rummaging around in the attic much to the annoyance of Beulah. "Whatever are you doing T.W.?" she queried.

"I'm just looking for good spots to shoot that will show the historical nature of the home ma'am."

"I see. Well please leave things exactly how you found them. I am gong downstairs to make some ice tea. Would either of you like some?"

"Nah, brought my own refreshments," Sadie responded as she pulled out her Jack Daniels from her purse and took a swig.

"Oh my!" Beulah gasped.

"Bill and Jack will probably want some though," Sadie added.

"Bill? Who's Bill?"

"I mean Zach," Sadie answered rolling her eyes toward T.W. signaling to him that she thought Beulah was crazy for not being able to get Bill's name straight.

Once Beulah left the attic, T.W. again started rummaging. He opened drawers in an old desk, felt under the seats of chairs, and searched through boxes. Bill couldn't have picked a better person than T.W. to do this task. After all, T.W. had been searching through garbage cans for years looking for hidden treasures.

"What are you doing T.W.?" asked Sadie as she was still standing in front of the arched window.

"Looking for treasure."

"And are you finding any?"

"Nothing. Not a thing!"

"Is everything all right up there?" Beulah called out from the kitchen three floors below. T.W. had been making so much noise that it drew Beulah's attention.

"Yes, everything is fine," Sadie yelled back. "T.W. is just looking for treasure."

Beulah's laughter could be heard all the way to the attic. "You people in show business!" She brought a tray with glasses of ice tea outside to Bill, Jack, Fripp, and Nathaniel. Jack was in the process of dismantling the equipment to do some shooting inside. Nathaniel was doing yard work. "Whatever is that man doing in my yard?" Beulah asked.

"Don't worry about him, Beulah," Bill excused. "Nathaniel just thought that since you have been so kind as to let us do some filming at your house, that he would do some yard work for you to repay the favor."

"My goodness, Zach, you certainly have an eclectic crew," Beulah sighed.

"We are getting ready to do some shooting inside Beulah. Do you think you could give us a tour?"

"By all means. Y'all drink up your ice tea and follow me."

"So Beulah," Jack asked, "have you ever found any treasure in this house?"

"What's all this talk about treasure Zach?" Beulah demanded. "Do you people think that there is treasure in my house?"

"No. No we don't," Fripp jumped in.

"Well we had heard that pirates might have buried or hidden treasure at 37 Meeting Street. So we thought that maybe they buried some here too," Bill explained.

"I can assure you that if there was any treasure here, Randolph and I would have found it. We have renovated this house top to bottom."

"And a fine job you've done of that Mrs. Cooper," Jack said with his usual charm.

"Well thank you, Jack."

Up in the attic, T.W. was rummaging through a pile of old books. He picked up one that seemed particularly old and blew the dust from the cover. "Hmm," he mumbled as he stuck the book in his coat. "Let's go and join the others Sadie."

T.W. and Sadie made their way to the basement where the rest of the crew was shooting film. They made their way floor by floor shooting film of all of the rooms and asking Beulah questions about each room. "I think we have enough for our documentary," Bill announced after the crew had filmed in the attic. "Thank you kindly for your hospitality Beulah."

"You're quite welcome Zach. Will I get a copy of the film when it's finished?"

"Definitely," Jack responded.

The crew loaded the equipment into a rented passenger van and headed back to Beaufort to first drop off Nathaniel, Sadie, and T.W, and then to head on to the Blue Dolphin Inn on Fripp Island. Fripp was driving. Sadie was riding shotgun. Jack and Nathaniel sat in the middle seat with T.W. and Bill occupying the back seat. "I wish you'd take a bath old man," Jack scolded T.W. "You stink. You are absolutely disgusting."

T.W. glared at the back of Jack's head. He reached into his coat and took out the book that he brought from Beulah's house. Holding the book in one hand he wiped the cover with his other hand then shook it toward the back of Jack's head. T.W. then handed the book to Bill and winked. Bill shoved the book down the back of his pants, under his shirt. Fripp and Jack were unaware of what had just taken place.

It was dark by the time that the crew reached Beaufort. Fripp drove to each of Sadie, Nathaniel, and T.W.'s homes. This was the first time that Bill had ever seen where these people lived.

Sadie lived above the submarine sandwich shop. Bill helped her out of the van and walked her up the stairs to her apartment. The staircase was narrow and had shifted so that one side of each step was higher than the other. The only light was a single bulb hanging from wires at the top of the stairs. When she opened the door, Bill could see that her only furnishings were a couch and a coffee table. The couch appeared to double as her bed. The apartment wasn't much more than four walls to look at. Bill now understood why she spent every day sitting on the bench down by the water.

Driving to a more prestigious part of town, Nathaniel Brown directed them to his house. "Th . . . Th . . . This is my house," Nathaniel stated proudly as they pulled up in front of a two story Victorian home. Even though it was dark, the street lights allowed Bill and Fripp to see that the lawns and shrubs were well manicured. What else would you expect at Nathaniel Brown's house?

Next, they drove to T.W. Wolfe's house. Although it too was in a prestigious part of town, the front yard was strewn with junk and garbage. T.W. exited the van and made his way toward the front door. As he turned a light on inside, Bill could see that the inside of T.W.'s house was filled with junk, antiques, artifacts, and of course garbage. From what Bill could see, there didn't appear to be anywhere to move or walk in the house.

After their day of filming, Bill felt closer to this eccentric group of characters. As he watched T.W. climbing over the junk in his house, Bill thought about how fond he was becoming of them, even with all of their quirks and odd behaviors.

Fripp drove to a friend that he knew in Beaufort who could develop film. Fripp spoke with the man at his door and when he returned to the van, he explained to Jack and Bill that the man would bring the film out to the Blue Dolphin Inn later that night.

"Here you go Bill," Fripp said handing Bill an envelope.

"What is it Fripp?"

"It's your new ID. That was the fellow who I said could set you up with a new ID. You have a driver's license, birth certificate, and a social security card. You are now officially Zachary Owens. I also arranged for you to have a summer job as a laborer with the public works department in Charleston. You start on Monday."

About midnight, the man showed up with the film. Fripp handed him an envelope with money in it. Jack, Bill, and Fripp went to cabin number three and set up a projector to watch the film.

"Ah, there's nothing here," Jack said discouragingly.

"Beulah did say that if there had been any treasure then her and her husband Randolph would have found it," Bill chimed up.

"Oh shut up! This has been a waste of time," Jack blurted.

"When you think about it Jack," Bill continued. "Dr. Alexander Dick sent his son Robert Keith and daughter Anne back with Dr. Pasteur. If they were staying at the Bull's house then Dr. Dick's treasure was at the house. I'm sure that he treasured his children more than any gold or silver."

"I said shut up!"

Fripp, seeing tension building between Bill and Jack broke in, "So, do you think now that there isn't a treasure, Jack?"

"Oh it's out there. I just don't know where and I don't know how to find it. This guy's the one who could lead us to it if he only could figure out the clues that have been left to him by his ancestors."

"Look Jack, I don't know what you are talking about. Until I met you, I never even heard of this treasure or my ancestors Alexander and William Dick. Why don't you just leave things alone?"

"That treasure is out there and I am going to find it," Jack insisted. "I will be watching you Bill," Jack warned as he stood up and shoved Bill's face toward the writing desk, "and if I find out that you have been holding out on me, you will be one sorry Canadian."

Bill felt a little bit of fear. He had never seen Jack get this angry before. Bill and Fripp looked at each other as Jack stormed out the cabin door, slamming it behind him. As Jack walked furiously toward the parking lot, he noticed a light on in the second floor of the main inn. He could see Sienna standing in the window. She had been watching what was going on in the cabin. Jack shook his fist in her direction, startled she jumped back from the window. The sound of tires speeding off could be heard in the distance as Sienna quickly made her way to cabin three.

"What's going on? I just saw Jack tear out of here."

"He's mad that we didn't find the treasure."

"Daddy, Bill, will you two stop wasting your time with this treasure," Sienna demanded. "It doesn't exist. If it did it would have been found long before now."

"Sienna is right, Bill. We have wasted a lot of time and involved other people in this treasure hunt of ours that could potentially put them in danger. At the very least, it has turned their lives upside down."

"Do you mean T. W. and Sadie?"

"Yes. And Nathaniel Brown and Beulah Cooper," Fripp added.

"You know what Fripp? You may be right," Bill conceded. "I really doubted BS Jack's whole story. Then he showed me the inscription on that Kentucky long rifle. I thought maybe there really is something to this."

"The problem is, Bill, anybody could have inscribed that rifle at any time."

"You're right."

"Listen to you two," Sienna said, exasperated. "You just won't quit talking about it!"

"My grandfather used to tell me a story about two children held captive in a tower," Bill spoke up. "In the story, the brother and sister were waiting for someone to set them free. I don't remember much about the story except for a couple of lines that go, '*Sister Anne, Sister Anne, do you see anybody coming? No but the wind's blowin' and the cock's crowin' and there's three men on horseback far, far away.*' T.W. gave me a journal that he found today at Beulah Cooper's house. I just want to read to you a couple of lines. Bill pulled out an old leather-bound journal from the civil war saddlebag that he had been using to carry his research papers around. The pages were yellowed and very fragile looking.

'*Mrs. Bull was a very kind and generous woman. Her hospitality to Anne and I is wonderful. Dr. Pasteur couldn't have found us a better place to stay in Charles Towne. Mrs. Bull is very protective of us both but especially Anne who is becoming a very beautiful young woman. With all of the British soldiers coming and going next door at 37 Meeting Street, Mrs. Bull prefers that Anne stay out of sight as much as possible. She sends us up to the attic whenever she thinks there might be trouble. Anne watches out the window looking for ships that are carrying our father's goods. She can see General Howe coming out of the entry at 37 Meeting Street to address his troops out on the street. He would usually do this just before ships were arriving at port. Anne often laughs at how much pomp and ceremony General Howe puts into this activity. Anne thinks he looks like a big peacock and would say look the cock is crowing again.*

At fifteen years old, I am still waiting for a growth spurt and I am too short to see out the window, so I ask Anne if she can see any ships coming. Anne is a few years older than me and about a head taller. Sometimes, using a spyglass that Mr. Bull had lent us, Anne could see the sails of our father's ships. Father had three horsemen painted on the main sails of his ships so that we would recognize his ships coming into the harbor.'

"That is amazing," Fripp grew excited. "Read more!"
"Okay, let me continue," Bill said.

'*Whenever we feel it is safe, Anne and I sneak out and make our way to the Provost Exchange and Dungeon. We stand in front of a tiny barred window that opens onto the street right at ankle height. Anne and I pretend to be carrying on a conversation. In actual fact she talks to McCafferty and tells him that our father's ships are coming into the harbor. Anne also takes food and drink for McCafferty and the others that are held in the dungeon. She stands against the Provost Exchange building so that her skirt completely covers the tiny window. Under her skirt, Anne carries food items and drinks that Mrs. Bull gave us. As she stands against the wall, McCafferty lifts the back of her skirt and takes the items to share with the other prisoners. Anne also wraps blankets around items as though she were carrying a baby. When we are sure that nobody is watching, I take the items from the blankets and pass them through the window.*

Anne often tells me that the stench coming up from the window is horrible and she didn't know how McCafferty and the others could stand the smell. I thought back to where McCafferty lived at Mary King's Close in Scotland and thought that this is nothing compared to the living conditions for some of the people there. "Father would be proud of you Anne," I encourage her. I know that she longs for our elegant home at Prestonfield House.'

McCafferty had a system for getting the cargo from our father's ships ahead of the British exchequer taking stock. In Scotland, my father had his treasure, the Templar's treasure, weapons and other items needed for the colonies stored in caskets at his underground distillery. Father knew that any casket that came from the underground would never be checked on its way out as people were afraid of the plague. McCafferty's trusted men in Scotland would load the caskets onto the ships at night in concealed chambers.

Once in Charles Towne Harbor, McCafferty and some of his men would sneak out at night through a hidden tunnel that they had built that went directly to the water. There, a boat would be waiting for them to go out to the ship and bring the caskets ashore. In the daylight, the caskets would be loaded on wagons and taken to various hiding spots in Charles Towne and Williamsburg. McCafferty would tell Anne and I how many caskets there were, what their contents were, and where they were going. Father wanted me to keep a record of this. The exchequer, although he did suspect that something was amiss was kept silent by McCafferty bringing in a couple of barrels of father's scotch, whiskey and substantial coin.

In order to meet the immediate needs of the patriots in and around Charles Towne, father had some of his wealth put into his whiskey barrels. Under the cover of night, I would assist McCafferty's men in taking these barrels and lowering them into the cistern at the college that Mr. Bull wanted to build.

I thoroughly enjoyed all of these secretive operations. I was used to it because of working with my father in the Edinburgh underground. Anne was not aware of our father's treasure and the Templar's treasure. She thought that all of the caskets and barrels were filled with supplies to help the colonies with the war. Father would list what was in each casket or barrel. McCafferty would remove that list from a hidden place on my father's ships and then when Anne and I would stand at the Provost and Exchange, in front of the window, McCafferty would slip the document into a concealed pocket on the underside of my sister Anne's skirt.

'When they needed supplies or funds, colonial leaders would leave a note for me at Mr. and Mrs. Bull's house. I would then meet them at the cistern at an appointed time during the night to retrieve whatever they needed or to direct them where to find one of the caskets.

One night, I was to meet Francis Marion at the cistern. I was told that they call him the Swamp Fox. I was enthused to be in the presence of such a legendary hero. Mr. Marion and a couple of his men brought a barrel filled with coins up from the cistern and then I gave him directions to where he could find several caskets that held the items they needed. "Obviously your father has taught you very well," Mr. Marion told me then he gave me one of his powder horns.

In all, father sent over 300 caskets and 600 whiskey barrels. Early on, many of the shipments went straight to the Village of Concord at the request of John Hancock. Mr. Hancock and Dr. Joseph Warren were part of a Committee of Safety that was collecting arms and supplies to get ready to fight against the British. Later, much of the supplies and arms were sent up to General Nathanael Greene and Lieutenant Colonel "Light Horse" Harry Lee when they were organizing at Charlotte, North Carolina. Father wanted me to keep track of where each casket and barrel was sent. The following is the location for each.'

Bill paused.

"Well?" Fripp asked. "Where? Where does it say they are?"

"The next few pages have been ripped out of the journal and then the journal continues with more of Robert Keith's story."

"Let me see that," demanded Fripp as he grabbed the journal. "You're right. Damn it. We are at a dead end again."

"Not necessarily Daddy," Sienna offered, now seeming interested in the potential of the treasure.

"What do you mean?"

"Well what if the colonists didn't take all of the barrels out of the cistern? Then there still could be some of the treasure there and it would also prove that all of this talk about treasure is true."

"Sienna is right Fripp. There still could be some of the barrels at the bottom of that cistern."

"Then we have to check it out," Fripp stated. "We just might find this treasure after all. "Tomorrow, let's go back to Charleston to see what we can discover. I'm going to turn in now," Fripp announced as he stood up and started toward the door. "Are you coming Sienna?"

"No Daddy. Not right yet. I think I'll sit and talk with Bill for a bit."

"Okay, but no hanky-panky you two!" Fripp commanded and winked at them.

The first thing that Sienna did once her father left was move in close to Bill and kiss him.

"Sienna, I was wondering what that big board is standing against the wall by the bed?"

"It's a bundling board."

"A what?"

"A bundling board. It was used a long time ago when people were courting so they could spend the night together and get to know each other without any you know—hanky panky."

"So how does it work?"

"Well," Sienna described, "it hooks into the headboard and runs down the middle of the bed separating the couple from each other. They are not to cross the board."

"That doesn't seem like much of a deterrent," Bill offered.

"Well the idea was also that some of the ladies would sew the couple into bundles, sort of like sleeping bags so that they actually couldn't touch each other."

"I see."

"Do you want to try it out?" Sienna smiled at Bill, standing up and taking his hand to draw him toward the bed.

"Your dad said no hanky panky and I don't think that board is going to keep me from you."

"No problem, my mom has some of the old bundle bags. I will go get her and she can sew us in." Sienna made her way toward the door of cabin number three, then turned around just before exiting, "And make sure you use the bathroom first, cause once you are sewn in you are stuck with me for the night." She grinned, tossing her hair as she walked away.

Once Louanne had put the bundling board in place and sewn the bundling bags enough so that Bill and Sienna could not engage in hanky panky, she turned out the lights, "I will see you two in the morning. Sweet dreams."

"Your mother is pretty cool, Sienna."

"Thanks. She is. But she's not my real mother you know. I was adopted."

Bill mustered his strength to struggle against the bundling bag enough to raise his head to look over the bundling board. He looked at Sienna's face.

"What is it Bill?" Sienna questioned.

"Oh just something that Sadie had said to me made me think for a minute," Bill explained as he laid his head back on his pillow. He thought to himself for a minute that Sadie gave up her baby girl almost eighteen years ago and Sienna was almost eighteen. What a coincidence.

Sienna moved and the bed squeaked. Bill then moved in mockery of the sound to get the bed to squeak again. Then Sienna did it and then Bill. Sienna giggled, "Kinda sounds like . . ."

"Like what?" Bill toyed with her.

"You know—hanky panky," she laughed. Bill followed along laughing with her.

Sienna and Bill talked into the night and fell asleep with the sound of the ocean waves in the background. Bill hadn't slept this peaceful in so long that he couldn't remember. He thought that he wouldn't mind sleeping beside this young woman for the rest of his life. He didn't dream of treasure that night. He dreamt of Sienna.

The Charleston Public Works

Early July 1976

Bill showed up early Monday morning at the Charleston Public Works. Although it was a great arrangement that Louanne had given him at The Blue Dolphin Inn, doing chores for a place to stay, he needed to make some money. Besides, he could still do the chores in the evenings and on weekends and that way he could be close to Sienna.

Along with five other young men, Bill was hired as a summer laborer. Their first morning on the job, the six men were told to stand against a wall in the shop and wait to be assigned to a crew. From where they were standing, the men could see over a counter and into the general office area where all of the foremen worked at their desks. There was also a superintendent working at his desk in an office with partial glass walls.

The superintendent got up from his desk and coming around the counter walked up and down past the six men looking them over like an officer inspects military troops. "You, you, and you," he commanded to the three strongest looking men, "you will be on the construction crew. You and you," he continued, "will be on maintenance. And you," he smiled at Bill, "will be doing valve maintenance with Rusty James."

Bill couldn't tell by the superintendent's smile if this was meant to be a good thing or a bad thing. The superintendent was a tall, slim man about forty years of age and spoke with a Massachusetts or Maine accent. When he spoke everyone listened and paid attention. Bill could tell that the superintendent was respected and not just because of his position. He had obviously earned the respect of all of his men.

Rusty James was an older man, almost at retirement age. He approached Bill and slurring his words said, "Here are the keys to truck number seventeen. It's parked across the road in the other yard. Go and get it and pick me up at the front of the building." Bill took the keys from Rusty's trembling hand. He knew that there was something wrong with Rusty but had never before come in contact with anyone who was suffering from Parkinson's disease. It turned out that Rusty had himself been the superintendent in his younger days but could no longer act in that capacity do to his deteriorating condition. Rusty had been a rugged man in his younger days. He was into hunting and fishing and had his own personal pickup truck rigged up with a makeshift camper on top.

Rather than turn Rusty out to pasture, the current superintendent kept Rusty on, doing valve maintenance. Rusty knew by heart where every water valve was in the City of Charleston. He could tell you where every water main was located and how deep it was. Rusty was a fountain of knowledge. The current superintendent used that as a reason to his superiors to keep Rusty on. In fact, Rusty had mentored the current superintendent. Bill thought that this was rather kind of the current superintendent and took a liking to him.

Truck number seventeen was equipped with all that Bill and Rusty needed for their work. It was, however, lacking in air conditioning and a radio that played music. Rusty had rigged up a transistor radio to a 6 volt battery which he kept on the dashboard on his side of the truck. Bill was to be the driver and Rusty was to be the passenger. Rusty would give the orders. Bill would take the orders. Rusty's radio was tuned in to a country and western station that played old, old country and western songs. Bill was not to touch the radio or change the station. As time went on, this became an irritation for Bill and a tug-of-war between the two men. "We'll head down town," Rusty told Bill.

As they approached a plaza on their way down town, Rusty told Bill to pull in. As Bill pulled in behind the plaza, he could see several Charleston Public Works trucks with no one in them.

"We'll go in here for a coffee," Rusty explained.

Inside, the small restaurant was half-filled with water workers. Bill and Rusty entered a booth beside two other workers. Rusty ordered a coffee and breakfast, so Bill did likewise. Bill thought to himself that this wasn't such a bad job. During breakfast, Rusty would bring his coffee cup to his mouth to drink. Sometimes he would take a sip and sometimes his hands were shaking too much so he put the cup back down before he spilled. It always took Rusty longer than the others to eat and finish his coffee so the others were long gone to their job sites before Rusty and Bill.

Stopping at Rose's restaurant was a daily routine. The superintendent knew that the crew did this, and most of the time he turned a blind eye. But every now and then the higher-ups would give him a hard time so he had to clamp down. One day, he showed up out in the front parking lot of the plaza and everybody scattered quickly out the back door. Everybody that is, except Rusty James and Bill. Rusty was way too slow and Bill wasn't about to run out on his partner.

Bill was sitting facing the front door and Rusty with his back to the door continued to eat his breakfast. Bill was anxious about what was about to happen, yet Rusty was as calm as could be. The superintendent walked over to their booth, took off his hat and sat down beside Bill. "Rusty, you know I'm gonna have to write ya up for this?"

"Yeah, I know. Do you want a coffee?"

"Sure."

Rusty called over toward the kitchen, "Rose, bring another coffee please, just milk, no sugar. And throw on a couple of eggs over easy, crisp bacon, and brown toast."

"You still remember you old codger," the superintendent chuckled. "I'm still gonna write ya up. I've got to write somebody up."

"Yeah, I know. Now let me and the kid here enjoy our breakfast."

Rusty, Bill, and the rest of the crew switched to another restaurant for about a week and then when the dust settled, they started going back to Rose's.

Valve maintenance was usually not a hard job. Rusty showed Bill the process. They had to find the valve, clean out the valve casing, grease the valve, make sure that it worked by putting the valve-key on it and turning it. Then they would hammer out a brass tag to number the valve and complete the paperwork. Once Rusty showed Bill the process, Bill did all the work and Rusty would sit in the truck, usually parked somewhere in the shade, listening to his country and western twang and doing the paperwork. That's when Bill would get a bit of a rest as it took Rusty longer to do the paperwork than it did for Bill to do the actual physical work. Rusty had to wait for a calm to come over him before he could write.

Every Thursday was pay day. Rusty had a routine and Bill was a captive to it. Just before lunch they would drive back to the shop to pick up their paychecks. Then they would drive over to Rusty's bank so Rusty could cash and deposit his cheque. Next they would drive to Kentucky Fried Chicken, buy lunch, and park somewhere under a shady live oak tree to eat their lunch and listen to Rusty's radio. Rusty was taking medication for his Parkinson's disease and it would sometimes make him sick. So Bill would have to drive somewhere for Rusty to throw up. If Rusty was feeling particularly ill, then Bill would drive him home and carry on doing a couple of valve jobs on his own. He would then drive by Rusty's house just before quitting time and pick him up so that they could book out together.

When Bill was doing these valve jobs on his own, he would change Rusty's radio to a station that he wanted to listen to. Out of respect for Rusty, Bill would always ensure that he set the radio back on Rusty's country station before he picked Rusty up again. There was the odd time that Bill forgot and Rusty would scowl at Bill when he got in the truck and he would immediately change the station back to country.

Quite often when Rusty and Bill were doing valve maintenance, they would come across a valve that they couldn't get the valve-key on. They would then have to dig this valve up to the water main and reset the casing. This would require getting a cut permit at city hall and arranging for locates. Bill didn't mind this as it gave him a break from working in the hot Charleston sun. The same arrangements had to be made when a valve was shown on a drawing but the casing wasn't at ground level and they had to go digging for it. Of course, Bill did the digging and Rusty sat in the shade. Bill really didn't mind though because he was learning a lot from Rusty by doing the work. They were also called on for emergencies and where the other laborers dug the holes and then stood back while their crew chief did the repair, Bill would dig the hole and then Rusty would stand at the top telling Bill what to do as Bill himself did the repair.

Rusty was almost always exactly right on where he said a valve would be. It might have been paved over or backfilled over but Rusty would just walk up to a site, look around, and tell Bill, "Dig here." Sure enough that would be exactly where the valve was. The two men didn't really talk that much as they went about their work. For one thing, talking was difficult for Rusty. He would drool and slur his words. So for the most part he stayed quiet. Bill didn't really have anything in common with Rusty so he pretty much kept quiet as well.

One particular hot and humid day, Bill and Rusty were required to dig up a missing valve. Rusty did his usual ritual of walking around, looking up and down the street and then walked over to a spot in the boulevard and pressed his foot down. "Dig here," he said.

Bill did as he had done many, many times before. He set a tarp out on the ground for the dug up earth to be placed. He brought his pick and shovel from the truck and began digging. As it got on about noon, Rusty wandered over from the truck where it was parked in the shade. Rusty gazed into a hole about six feet wide by six feet long and about five feet deep that Bill had dug by hand in the heat and humidity. "I don't think it's here Rusty!"

"Oh it's there alright. Dig this way a little more."

Bill found the water main and kept tunneling along it looking for the valve. It was nowhere to be found. About mid-afternoon, Rusty walked over to the hole again. It was obvious that he had been having a nap. "Come on up outa there."

"Come with me," Rusty said as he walked across the street. Rusty was holding a drawing which he then turned right-side up. Rusty pressed his foot down on the ground, "Dig here."

Bill took a couple of shovels and then on the third shovel full he hit the top of the valve casing. Bill was angry. He was very angry. But he didn't yell at Rusty, or say anything nasty to him. He didn't even say a word to him. Bill just went on about his work of doing the maintenance on the valve and bringing the casing up to ground level. When he was finished with that valve, Bill went and backfilled the huge hole that he had spent most of the day digging. It was almost quitting time when Bill made his way back to the truck. Rusty had slipped away to a nearby store and bought two ice cold Cokes, one for Bill and one for himself. "Here son."

"Thanks," Bill barely had the word out and he was chugging the cold drink down. "That's good," he said. Bill sat there for a minute before he noticed that Rusty had tuned the radio station from his country station to something modern. Bill took this as an apology from Rusty. When Bill noticed the station had been changed, he looked over at Rusty and Rusty smiled. Everything was now okay between them.

Usually the crews would arrive back at the shop about 20 minutes before quitting time so that each crew chief could complete his paperwork. As the crews pulled in they would park their truck in the yard across from the shop and then walk across the road. All of the crews did this except one. The crew chief for that crew was a particular big man. He towered over all of the rest of the workers and was muscular as well. They called him Dutch. Bill didn't know why, because Dutch spoke with a Massachusetts or Maine accent the same as the superintendent. Dutch always made his laborer drive him right to the office door and then go park his truck for him. The six laborers usually found themselves standing against the wall waiting for the quitting signal. If Dutch hadn't had his laborer park his truck yet then he would pick on one laborer, Vijay, who happened to be of East Indian descent. Dutch would constantly call him names and make fun of him. Dutch would tell Vijay to go and park his truck and did so in a degrading manner. Pretty much everyone laughed, but their laughter was out of fear of Dutch rather than finding his jokes humorous.

One day, Dutch was carrying on his usual mockery of Vijay, when Bill accidentally said out loud, "Why don't you just leave him alone?"

"What did you say, Shrimp?" Dutch bellowed.

The entire shop went silent. Bill's heart was in his throat. He was afraid, yet he knew that he needed to stick up for Vijay because no one else would. "I said why don't you just leave him alone."

All eyes turned to Dutch, anticipating his response. He threw his keys across the room just barely missing Bill's head and hitting the wall behind him, "Go park my truck!"

Bill was in a quandary. If he picked up the keys and went out to park Dutch's truck, then Dutch had just put him in his place and would continue harassing Vijay. On the other hand, Dutch was a crew chief and deserved respect. But then again, he wasn't Bill's crew chief. Yet still, Dutch could probably crush Bill using one hand.

"Park it yourself!" Bill stated firmly.

Dutch stood up from his desk and quickly came around the counter approaching Bill. The superintendent was now watching. Dutch glared into Bill's eyes, "I said go park my truck."

Bill tried not to show the fear that he was feeling. He thought that at any moment Dutch was going to punch him in the face. Trying not to cringe Bill firmly stated again, "I said go park it yourself."

Dutch was now fuming. He bent down and picked up his keys. Bill was expecting Dutch to ram them down his throat. Dutch turned to Vijay, "You go park my truck or your friend here will regret that he stuck up for you."

"I'll park your damn truck," a soft, shaky voice came from the crew chief's side of the counter. It was Rusty James. Even with all of his disabilities and struggles, Rusty still had the respect of all of the men. Dutch wasn't about to take him on. Instead, he stormed out of the shop and parked his own truck.

There was silence in the shop as everyone was trying to digest what had just happened. The superintendent walked to his office door and looking over to the wall where the six laborers were standing bellowed out, "Owens, my office, now!" Bill had been using the name Zachary Owens as the Charleston Police were still looking for William Dick in relation to the stolen rifle incident at the Edmonston-Alston House.

The superintendent had sat back down behind his desk. Bill stood almost at attention in front of him. "Owens, you know that was insubordination?"

"Yes sir, I do."

"Then you also know that I have to let you go."

"I understand."

"I'm sorry to have to do that son because you are the only one that I have found in recent years that has had the patience to work with Rusty James. I know what goes on—that you do all of the work. Almost everyone else that I have assigned to Rusty complains and asks to be transferred, but not you. It will be disappointing to Rusty."

"Yes sir."

"One more thing son."

"Yes sir?"

"You sure have got some guts sticking up to my brother, Dutch, like that."

"Your brother?"

"Yes, Dutch is my younger brother. I have never seen anybody around here stick up to him. It was good to see it. But rules are rules. Your final pay will be sent to you. All the best Owens." The superintendent stood up and shook Bill's hand. Everyone was watching through the glass.

Bill made his way back around the counter and past the lineup of the other 5 laborers. Everyone knew that he was being let go as Bill made his way toward the door and it wasn't quite quitting time yet. As Bill opened the door to leave, the laborers and crew chiefs started to clap and cheer, "Way to go, Owens." "You showed him." "Hang in there kid."

As far as Bill was concerned, it wasn't a bad thing that had just happened. He could now spend a little more time with Sienna and trying to find the treasure. He had made some money to keep him going for a while and he had made another friend, Rusty James.

THE COLLEGE OF CHARLESTON

LATE JULY 1976

The College of Charleston, which was the oldest university or college in South Carolina, was founded in 1770. This fact fit right in with the timeline of Jack Falstaff's story that Dr. Alexander Dick started shipping his treasure and the Templar's treasure over to the colonies in 1771. Randolph Hall was a very impressive structure, six massive columns sat above five large archways. There was a clock centered at the top of the building. Staircases led up each side to a balcony where the entry to the building was. This gave Randolph Hall a regal aura about it. The cistern which was in front of Randolph Hall was massive. It had a walkway leading up to it from George Street and then another walkway which went on toward Randolph Hall. The cistern courtyard itself was very mystic with huge oak trees creating a natural ceiling. Rays of sunlight shone through the branches.

Bill, Sienna, and Fripp sat on the edge of the cistern watching college students and tourists come and go. A ray of sunlight was shining directly on Sienna and Bill thought that it emphasized the beauty of her face and hair. Sienna noticed Bill looking at her and smiled. She took his hand.

Cistern—College of Charleston, South Carolina

"Well Bill," Fripp broke the silence. "I don't suppose the College of Charleston would like it if we just started digging up the ground above the cistern here, might cause a bit of a disturbance."

"Daddy," Sienna offered. "There is a problem."

"Well I know there is a problem Sienna. We can't just start digging up the grounds here."

"Daddy, the cistern wasn't here in 1771. Many of the buildings that make up the College were not constructed until after the American Revolution. In fact this famous cistern courtyard which sits in front of Randolph Hall was not constructed until 1857. So really where could treasure be hidden here? What cistern was Robert Keith Dick writing about in his journal? Obviously not this one. Surely there had to be some cistern in existence at the college in 1771."

"I know who we can ask to help," Fripp responded, "the Thompson twins."

Frank Thompson and his brother Paul were unbelievable characters. If they didn't really exist, nobody would believe that they did. In their younger days, Frank and Paul ran a thriving well digging and drilling business. They could find water sources anywhere. If Frank and Paul couldn't find it then it wasn't there. They also did maintenance on septic systems and cisterns.

After their father died, the twins moved into an old house on Cumberland Street with their mother. Neither of the twins had married. Once they moved in with their mother, their behavior became strange. They stopped bathing and they lost most of their business. The twins let the old house become run down to the point where the city had to condemn it. Although it was the general thought that they had boat loads of money, Frank, Paul, and their mother packed what they could into a Lincoln Continental and used it as their new accommodations. They would spend their days driving all around Charleston. They ate and slept in the vehicle. They changed clothes in there as well.

In time, the twins' mother passed away. They actually kept driving around for several days with their dead mother in the car before they did anything about it. Once their mother was buried, Frank and Paul purchased a smaller vehicle. They apparently walked into the car dealership and paid cash. People wondered why they didn't just fix up their house which was sitting empty. So, Frank and Paul continued spending their days driving around. Whenever, they would go into a grocery store or coffee shop they would leave behind an offensive odor. One nice thing that could be said about the twins was that they were extremely polite.

Fripp had grown to know the twins and actually let them use the facilities at the Alvermay Inn.

The following day Bill, Sienna, and Fripp met with Frank and Paul Thompson at the cistern courtyard. Once again students and tourists were coming and going. Today however, this small group was getting the attention of the crowds. This of course was due to the scruffiness of Frank and Paul.

"Yup," Paul stated, "your daughter's right Fripp. This cistern and Randolph Hall were not here in 1771."

"Was there any cistern in existence in 1771 for the College of Charleston?" Fripp asked with a sound of desperation in his voice.

"What do you say Frank?" Paul asked turning to his brother.

"Glebe Street."

"Yup, Glebe Street."

"What's on Glebe Street?" Bill asked.

"Reverend Robert Smith was an Anglican priest from England," Sienna articulated. "He became the reverend for Saint Philip's and eventually he became the first Episcopalian Bishop in South Carolina. In 1770 Reverend Smith had a house built at the back end of the church property which is now known as Glebe Street. He was sympathetic to the patriots and before the actual college buildings were constructed, Reverend Smith taught classes in his house."

"So in effect," Bill surmised, "Reverend Smith's house was the college in 1771. Do you fellows know which house it was?"

"Yup," Paul answered, "it is number six Glebe Street. That's her down the road yonder. She's a two storey, brick, Georgian style. She's got a brick wall around her with an iron gate."

"Daddy, they use that house now for the president of the college."

"Paul," Fripp asked, "Do you know where the cistern is for the house?"

"Frank?" Paul responded turning to his brother.

"Yup, I can locate it."

"He can locate it. Why do you want to find an old cistern from 1771?" Paul asked Fripp.

"We have reason to believe that there could be some whiskey barrels down there that contain treasure."

"Not true Fripp. That's an old wives tale," Frank responded.

"Yup, an old wives tale," Paul added.

"Well will you help us to find the cistern?" Bill pleaded.

"We can. We will," Frank answered.

"Yup, we can. We will," Paul added.

"We will meet you there tonight right at sundown," Frank instructed.

"Yup, right at sundown."

"Okay," Fripp agreed.

The Thompson twins made their way down the path toward George Street. Passersby gave odd looks toward the twins. Bill, Sienna, and Fripp walked around the cistern and sat facing Randolph Hall. Bill Glanced over toward the entry to Randolph Hall. He thought that he had seen BS Jack standing in one of the archways. "Fripp, did you tell Jack that we were meeting the Thompson twins here?"

"No, I did tell Kitty where I could be found. I left her to look after the bar."

"Is Jack still staying at the Alvermay?"

"Sure," Fripp answered. "He has room number three, as always. BS Jack is a good paying customer."

"Just be careful Fripp," Bill counseled. "I don't trust him."

Later that day as the sun went down, Bill, Sienna, and Fripp walked up East Bay Street to Wentworth Street and then turned north on Glebe Street. Sienna took Bill's hand as they walked. Fripp couldn't help but notice how close Bill and Sienna were becoming. As they started up Glebe Street, the three could see the Thompson twins' service truck up ahead. This was the first time in years that their service truck had been put to use. The truck had a sign on the tank which read,

'Thompson Cistern & Septic Pumping & Repair'
'Well Digging and Drilling'

Fripp thought that this was good that the twins brought their truck as then they likely wouldn't draw attention from the neighbors.

"Found it Fripp," Frank said as if in victory.

"Yup, found it," Paul added.

"Already?" Bill asked. "You guys are good."

"The best," Frank announced.

"Yup, the best," Paul confirmed.

"Is anybody home?" Sienna questioned.

Frank motioning to the house across the road responded, "Neighbor said they've gone on vacation. The cistern is straight over there beside the garden wall. Paul has already uncovered the lid."

"Yup, uncovered the lid."

All five walked over to the excavation. Bill and Fripp grabbed a shovel each and began to pry off the lid. There was still water in the old cistern which emitted a stagnant odor when the lid came off. Five faces peered down into the darkness.

"I guess you are going down Bill," Fripp decided.

Sienna looked at Bill and the five of them chuckled. He was the youngest male and by an unspoken process of seniority deciding, everyone knew that it had to be him. Bill himself knew it. Frank grabbed a harness from the truck and Paul helped Bill into the harness. Frank and Paul set up a tri-pod to lower Bill into the cistern. The opening itself wasn't much larger than the width of Bill's shoulders.

As Bill descended through the opening his head just disappearing below the surface of the ground, Frank warned, "Watch out for snakes!"

"Yup, snakes," Paul echoed.

"Now you tell me! My feet are just reaching the water line. It's pitch black down here. Can you send me down a light?"

They lowered Bill further until only his neck and head were above the water line. "I still can't see or feel anything other than the water. Should I go down deeper Frank?"

"I wouldn't. I told you there is no treasure. It's just an old wives tale," Frank answered.

"Give me some slack on the line," Bill called up. "I am going to go under the water."

Frank slackened the line enough so that Bill could swim down to about eight feet below the water line. It was dark and scummy. Bill swam around at the bottom of the cistern and bang—his head hit something hard. Even though he had goggles on he still couldn't see what it was he hit. Bill came back up to the surface for air. Gasping, he yelled up, "There is something down there. I am going back down to see."

Bill descended again to the bottom of the cistern where he felt the hard object. Now with lungs full of air he could take a little more time investigating. He felt his way around the object. It was about two feet tall and cylindrical. Bill came back to the surface, "It's a barrel. Throw me down a rope."

He took the rope down with him and tied it around the barrel. Back at the surface of the water, Bill had Frank and Paul haul him up. Then all three men hauled the barrel up.

"Well I'll be!" Fripp exclaimed. "I never would have thought that the treasure actually existed."

"We don't know that it is treasure Daddy. It's just a barrel."

"What else would it be?" Fripp questioned rhetorically.

"Let's get this back to the Alvermay and look at it closer," Bill suggested.

"That sounds like a plan," Sienna concurred, "and you need to get rid of those clothes and take a shower."

Fripp, Frank, and Paul put the barrel on the truck and climbed in. "I will walk back with Bill," Sienna offered.

Bill went upstairs to his room and grabbed some clean clothes. He walked down the hall to the washroom and removing his clothes, he passed them out the door to Sienna who was waiting with a garbage bag. "These are going right in the garbage," she stated.

When Bill finished his shower and put on his clean clothes, he started to head towards the top of the stairs. He heard some noise coming from Jack's room so he thought he would confront him to find out if that actually had been Jack watching them at the College of Charleston earlier in the day.

Normally Bill would knock on the door and wait for a response but he wanted to catch Jack off-guard. Bill turned the handle slowly and flung the door open. What he saw he couldn't have prepared himself for. Here were Jack and Erica naked in Jack's bed.

"Erica?"

"Bill, I can explain!" Erica pleaded as she grabbed a sheet to wrap around herself. Jack had already jumped up and was pulling on some pants.

"There's no need to explain Erica. We aren't together anymore. You dumped me. You can be with whoever you choose."

"I'm sorry Bill," Erica apologized.

"No need to apologize Erica. I've moved on too. I've met someone wonderful who I love very much. But I thought that you left Charleston."

Erica looked over toward Jack with an expression on her face that said we should tell him.

"Bill," Jack started, "Erica and I have been seeing each other for over a year now."

"What? What are you talking about?"

"Oh come on mate. Surely you aren't that stupid or that naïve. Think about it man. Erica and I, in my room, do you think that it's just a coincidence that we're together?"

"Jack was a teaching assistant for one of my history courses," Erica explained. "When we started going out I was going to tell you."

"But I wouldn't let her," Jack cut in. "I had heard a legend about the Dick family and treasure that may be here in Charleston so I had Erica continue to date you and get you to come down here to Charleston."

"So when you met me outside Poogan's Porch?" Bill asked.

"All a set-up."

"I can't believe that you would do this to me Erica. I thought that we were best friends."

"I made her do it Bill. Don't blame her."

"She had a choice."

"I'm sorry Bill," Erica repeated.

"Well the joke's on you two. We did find something but obviously you two won't be sharers in it."

"Yeah, I'm sure that you did!" Jack sarcastically remarked.

"Look out your window Jack. Fripp is out in the alley, cleaning off a barrel that we found in a cistern on Glebe Street."

"Huh. That's it. Woopdy-doo!" Jack expressed as he looked out the window of his room that overlooked the alley. "There's a lot more than that out there and I am going to find it. As a matter of fact Bill you better hold on tight to that one barrel that you did find."

"Stop it Jack. Haven't we caused enough harm to Bill already?" Erica cried.

"Not near enough. He wouldn't even know about the treasure if it wasn't for my research. I've come down here to Charleston for the last three summers, researching, investigating, interviewing, and digging. That treasure is mine. I deserve it."

"Jack, you're scaring me!" Erica whimpered.

"Let's get out of here Erica!" Jack commanded as he threw his clothes and belongings into a suitcase.

"Good-bye Erica. I hope you find what you're looking for," Bill stormed out of the room and down the stairs.

Bill was sitting in the bar downstairs explaining to Sienna what had happened when he heard Jack and Erica come down the stairs and exit through the front door. Moments later, Bill saw Erica's Volkswagen bug head south on East Bay Street.

"Bill! Bill!" Fripp called from the alley.

Bill and Sienna jumped up and ran out to the alley to find Fripp lying on the ground with a large welt on his left cheek. "Daddy! What happened?"

"They took the barrel. Jack and his girlfriend took the barrel. He punched me and knocked me to the ground and then ran off with the barrel."

Frank and Paul Thompson had been there as well but they weren't about to get involved in any violence. So they had just watched the whole thing. "Yup, took the barrel," Paul said.

Bill helped Fripp get on his feet. "I had the barrel open Bill. It was filled with gold and silver coins. I saw it with my own eyes. It was unbelievable Bill."

"What should we do Fripp? Should we go after them?"

"Let them go. They will find us again soon enough. These pages were in the top of the barrel, sealed in a watertight container," Fripp said holding up several pages that looked like they had been ripped from a book.

"Do you think that they are from Robert Keith Dick's journal Fripp?"

"Let's go inside and take a look."

Fripp, Bill, Sienna, Frank, and Paul sat down at one of the tables in the bar area. Fripp had brought a light over so that they could see better. The pages didn't continue exactly from where they had left off reading at the Blue Dolphin Inn but it was obvious that they were missing pages from Robert Keith Dick's journal.

'*Mrs. Bull took Anne and I with her today when she went to visit her friend Mrs. Eveleigh over at number thirty-nine Church Street. It is a beautiful house and Anne fell in love with it. George and Mrs. Eveleigh have a little girl named Catherine who although much younger than Anne and I amused us with her games. She especially liked playing hide-and-seek. Catherine showed us a secret staircase that went from a secret room below the house up to a closet in the drawing room. I thought that this might be quite useful to us in the future.*

Doctor Pasteur came to visit today. He was concerned about the Holy Grail being so easily accessible in Williamsburg so he brought it to me for safe keeping. I have been concerned lately since the British have occupied Charleston. Many of the Patriots have been imprisoned in the Provost Dungeon with McCafferty and the other Scots who are posing as pirates. Thankfully, McCafferty had built the tunnel from the Tavern to the dungeon and on out to the Cooper River in advance of allowing himself to be captured as a pirate. This has provided such an escape from the hardships of the prison for the patriots and has allowed us to move supplies in and out even during the occupation.'

"These are obviously pages from Robert Keith's journal. What tavern he is talking about?" Bill wondered.

"The Alvermay was the only tavern close by to the Exchange at that time," Sienna answered.

"Then there has to be a tunnel from the Alvermay to the Exchange." Bill stated.

"There can't be," Fripp responded. "I've never seen anything that remotely resembles a tunnel."

"You need Rusty James," Frank said.

"Yup, Rusty James," Paul echoed.

"I know Rusty James. I can get him to help us," Bill offered.

The Alvermay Inn & Tavern

Charleston

Early August 1976

"I tell you Bill. There is no tunnel from here to the Dungeon. I've owned this place for twenty years and never seen anything that remotely resembles a secret passage or hidden tunnel."

"Rusty James here can find any underground water passage that exists," Bill exhorted. "Let him do his stuff."

Bill, Fripp, and Rusty James walked out onto Exchange Street. Rusty was carrying two copper rods that were about three feet long each having a ninety degree bend at about the one foot mark. Positioning himself on Exchange Street at East Bay and facing the Cooper River, Rusty held a copper rod in each hand with the short ends pointing down toward the ground and the long ends protruding from his hands and pointing toward the Cooper River. Rusty waited for a calm in his shaking body, then he began to walk east toward the Cooper River. When he had made his way about thirty feet, the copper rods suddenly turned themselves so that the one in his left hand was pointing toward the Old Exchange and the one in his right hand was pointing toward the Alvermay. As Rusty James continued walking, the copper rods swung back around parallel to each other pointing toward the Cooper River again.

"There is something down there alright," Rusty James said.

"There can't be," Fripp said. "I have never seen anything."

"The rods don't lie. There is something down there," Rusty James restated.

"Let's go inside and look around Fripp," Bill suggested.

"How old is that freezer, Fripp?" Bill asked pointing to a large walk-in deep freeze.

"I don't know. It was here when I bought the place. It still works good. So I just kept it."

"Have you ever moved it?" Bill asked.

"Never had a need to. Are you thinking that there might be a tunnel below it? We are going to need more than you and I to move that sucker. It is heavy as all get out."

"Let's get T.W. and As Far As to help," Bill suggested. "They already know that we are looking for treasure."

"That's a good idea Bill. We can drive to Beaufort tonight and then come back here tomorrow with them. I can get Kitty to watch the bar for me tonight."

Fripp, Bill, T.W., and As Far As, moved the freezer from its position. They stood looking at the concrete floor which was uniform throughout the entire kitchen. "You see Bill," Fripp said referring to the concrete floor. "There is no tunnel, no secret passageway. Are you satisfied?"

"Okay Fripp. You're right. Let's push this freezer back."

As T.W. stepped toward the freezer, he slipped on some ice that had fallen.

"Are you okay?" Fripp asked helping T.W. to his feet.

"As far as, he looks okay. As far as, he broke the floor," Nathaniel expressed. Beside T.W. was a broken chunk of concrete exposing wooden floorboards underneath.

Bill looked at Fripp, who looked at T.W., who looked at As Far As. There was excitement on their faces. "We need a hammer Fripp."

Fripp went out to the alleyway to look for something to use to hammer out the concrete. He returned with a piece of iron bar and began to thrust it at the concrete floor. After a few minutes, he grew tired and handed the iron bar to Bill to continue. Bill and Fripp switched every few minutes to give each other a break. As pieces of concrete broke away, T.W. would clear them.

After about two hours of banging away chunks of concrete, Fripp and Bill had exposed an area of floorboards about six feet by six feet. Fripp tapped on the floorboards. It sounded hollow underneath. They then continued smashing the boards with the iron bar until they had an opening big enough for a man to fit through. A spiral staircase was visible. It had stone steps and brick walls.

"I'll get a flashlight," Fripp said going out to the bar.

"As far as, I'm not going down there."

"I am!" T.W. exclaimed. "I haven't waited all these years to just stand back here and watch."

The winding stairway descended about twenty feet. The stone steps, although not having been used for many years were well worn. At the bottom of the stairway was a small tunnel of about six feet which entered into a cavern-like room. The room was about twelve feet wide and twelve feet long with a height of about seven feet. It too had brick walls with a stone floor. The walls and ceiling were arched in order to support the ground above. At the east side of the room was another tunnel exiting the room. Straight ahead to the north side was also a tunnel. The room and the tunnels were covered in cobwebs.

There was a very plain looking wooden desk in the middle of the room. On top of the desk were a lantern and a log book. There were a few other books sitting in a pile on the desk. All had been gathering dust for almost two hundred years. An old, wooden chair sat behind the desk and a second lantern was hanging on a hook above the desk. Beside the desk sat a barrel. The letters on it could barely be made out but Fripp was able to determine that they read in part, 'Zachary Owens, Williamsburg, Virginia.'

"I bet this is where McCafferty sat and expedited the shipments from Dr. Alexander Dick?" Bill wondered out loud.

"And I'll bet that's McCafferty!" Fripp exclaimed as he shone his flashlight into a corner of the room. Perched in the corner was the skeleton of what was once a very tall man. His clothing was almost deteriorated. On his right side was a flintlock pistol. On his left side was an empty bottle of scotch whiskey and some papers. "It's the Mad Scotsman!"

"Fripp, Fripp, Fripp, I told you. There are no such things as ghosts." Bill picked up the papers, "Shine your light on these a minute Fripp."

'May 14, 1780

Dear Young Robert Keith,

I am sorry to have failed you and your father. Although the Templar's treasure has been secured and hidden, I did not get all of the barrels of your father's money out in time before the British have taken over Charles Towne. My men and I have done our best. The documents for the latest shipment are with this letter. I'm afraid that much of it has fallen into British hands.

Tomorrow, my men and I are to be taken to White's Point and we are to be hanged as pirates. I cannot face such a dishonorable death. I am no pirate. My men all know their fate and have reconciled themselves to the fact that there is no way out. I have told them that I intend to shoot myself instead of letting the British hang me.

I want to thank your father, Dr. Alexander Dick. It is only because of him that I have had the opportunities to make something of my life. He took me under his wing when I was a ruffian and taught me to read and write. He trusted me to watch over his riches. Your father is a real gentleman, a hero to this war. It is a shame that people will never know that.

Even while imprisoned here at the Provost, I have had the opportunity, by use of these tunnels, to get out and see some of the new world. That is a privilege that I never would have enjoyed without your father's help. I would still be stuck in the underground city of Edinburgh.

Take good care of your sister Anne.

Sincerely,
John McCafferty'

"Let's go this way Fripp," T.W. motioned toward the tunnel at the north side of the room.

Holding the flashlight, Fripp led the way with Bill following and T.W. in tow. They cautiously moved forward at a very slow pace. Fripp would shine the light in front of them, then to the floor and the walls. They thought to themselves that it was almost two hundred years ago since anyone had been down here. They were excited and scared at the same time. After only a minute or so, their journey ended by coming straight into a brick wall.

"This must be the wall of the dungeon Bill," Fripp said.

"That makes sense. We basically would have just crossed under the road from the Alvermay."

"So there's nothing here," T.W. said disappointedly.

"Well this tunnel itself is amazing T.W.," Fripp offered. "It shows that there is some truth to what Robert Keith wrote in his journal. It means that quite likely some of the treasure is out there somewhere."

"Let's check the other tunnel!" T.W. exclaimed running back toward the cavern-like room.

Fripp and Bill followed behind but still walked slowly and cautiously. The three then entered the tunnel that ran to the east. This tunnel was much longer but did end after about two hundred feet.

"Another dead-end," T.W. expressed with exasperation.

"This must be where they brought in the coffins and barrels that were filled with treasure from the ships on the Cooper River," Bill said. "I wonder how many times McCafferty and his men went in and out of this tunnel?"

Bill had been carrying the iron bar that the men had used to break away the concrete and the floorboards. "Give me that," T.W. demanded, taking the iron bar from Bill. T.W. began to flail away at the brick wall which ended the tunnel.

"Easy T.W.," Bill counseled. "We don't know how safe these walls are. We don't want to get buried down here."

T.W. continued flailing at the wall with all his strength. "My whole life," he yelled. "My whole life," he repeated.

Just then a spurt of water started to come through the wall at the point where T.W. was hitting it.

"C'mon T.W. We better get out of here," Fripp warned as he started to back up down the tunnel.

T.W. paid no heed. He just kept swinging the iron bar. Water started to now gush from the opening. "C'mon T.W.," Bill yelled.

Suddenly the entire brick wall at the end of the tunnel came crashing down on top of T.W. The tunnel was starting to fill with water from the Cooper River. Bill grabbed T.W. by the coat-sleeve and tried to pull him from under the brick wall. By now, T.W. was under water and Bill was standing waist deep. Bill kept trying, pulling on T.W. Thoughts of his father came to Bill, "I'm not going to let you go too," Bill yelled.

T.W., realizing that Bill's efforts were useless, pulled his arm away and pushed on Bill's leg signaling him to go and save himself. Bill moved through the water as fast as he could and caught up to Fripp in the cavern. Fripp was just starting up the stairway with the water quickly chasing him.

Soon the water filled the tunnel, the cavern and found its level somewhere on the stairway.

Fripp was resting on the steps as Bill rounded a bend. "Well nobody will be going down there ever again," he said as he tried to get his breath.

Bill Helped Fripp to his feet and they climbed the last few steps together.

"Wh . . . wh . . . where's T.W.?"

"T.W. didn't make it, Nathaniel."

Fripp, Bill, and As Far As pushed the freezer back into position over the opening. There was a feeling of remorse among the three of them.

FORGIVENESS

After T.W.'s death in the secret tunnel between the Alvermay and the Provost Dungeon and Jack stealing the only bit of treasure that the group had found, Bill and Fripp decided to leave off searching for the treasure. Jack and Erica had moved on now as far as anybody knew. Fripp returned to running the Alvermay. Bill moved back to the Blue Dolphin Inn where he could be closer to Sienna. Nathaniel Brown had developed such an attachment to Bill that Nathaniel's family allowed him to move out to the Blue Dolphin Inn as well. Nathaniel was in his glory as Louanne assigned him to the grounds maintenance. Bill even brought Nathaniel's bike out to the Inn so that he would feel more comfortable, riding his bike from job site to job site.

The early days of August were particularly hot. Bill was thankful to be near the ocean where the breezes kept things a little cooler. He couldn't help thinking about Sadie and wondering if Sadie was actually Sienna's mother. They looked so much alike and it was odd that Sienna had been given up for adoption at about the time that Sadie gave up her baby girl. Bill approached Nathaniel Brown's parents, who, through their prominence and contacts in Beaufort were able to gain access to the adoption records. Sure enough, it appeared that in fact Sadie was Sienna's mother.

"Louanne," Bill said as he approached the porch where Louanne had been sitting removing peas from their pods. "I think that I might know who Sienna's birth mother is." Bill was feeling particularly nervous not knowing what reaction that Louanne would have to this. His stomach was in his throat.

"Uh huh," Louanne responded slowly and guardedly.

"I think that she is this woman who I met in Beaufort. Her name is Sadie."

"And I suppose that you think they should meet?"

"Actually, I want to know what you think, Louanne."

When Bill said this, Louanne changed her demeanor. She now engaged herself in the idea. "I think that we should ask Sienna," Louanne responded. "If Sienna's okay with it then I'm okay with it."

Later that evening after supper, Bill asked Sienna if she wanted to meet her birth mother. Sienna's immediate reaction was to look at Louanne to see how she was reacting. "I'm okay with it Sienna," Louanne encouraged.

"But Mom, you are the only mother that I have ever known. Nobody else could replace you. I love you too much."

"That's all I really need to hear Sienna. I don't feel that I'd be losing you. This would just be another page in your life that you can turn."

"I would like to meet her and ask why she gave me up. I just can't see how a mother can do that to her baby."

"Yes Sienna, I agree. But we don't know people's circumstances. If you would like to meet her then Bill can arrange it. Would you do that Bill?"

"Yes, I will. How about I bring her out to the Blue Dolphin if she is willing?"

"That would be great," Sienna responded. "Then Mom can meet her too."

The next morning Bill went down to the park at the waterfront in Beaufort. He sat down on the bench where he had first met T.W. and then Sadie and then Nathaniel Brown. Before long, Sadie approached and sat down beside him, once again clunking her knitting bag on the bench. She pulled out her mickey of Jack Daniels and as she was putting it to her mouth, Bill put his hand on her forearm to stop her from drinking, "Sadie, how would you feel about meeting your daughter?"

"Yeah right," Sadie said as she continued to take a swig.

Bill again put his hand on Sadie's forearm to take the bottle away from her mouth. "I'm serious Sadie. I know who your daughter is and where she is."

"Bill, if this is true . . . It better be true. I couldn't take the disappointment. If this is true then I swear on this bottle I will stop drinking."

"You are coming back to the Blue Dolphin Inn with me Sadie. Is there anything that you need to get from your apartment?"

"Nothing Bill. I have nothing."

Louanne had prepared an early supper for Sadie's visit. Upon arriving back at the Blue Dolphin Inn, Bill took Sadie to his cabin so that she could shower and clean up. He had borrowed some clean clothes for Sadie from Louanne, who was about the same size.

When Sadie was all set, Bill and her nervously made their way up to the main cottage. As they entered the kitchen, Sienna and Louanne looked up from the kitchen table. Louanne could not get over the resemblance between Sienna and Sadie.

"This is Sadie," Bill said. "And this is Sienna and Sienna's mother Louanne." Bill was sure to make that point clear so that Louanne did not feel that she was being replaced in any way.

"Welcome Sadie," Louanne said.

"Pleased to meet you both," Sadie responded.

Sienna kept staring at Sadie like she was looking in a mirror. Sadie had cleaned up really well and in fact had a very striking beauty to her just like Sienna. "Are you my mother? I mean my birth mother," Sienna asked while turning to Louanne.

"Bill seems to think so."

"I have to know. Why did you give me up?"

"I didn't want to. My parents made me. I was young. My being pregnant was an embarrassment to them and their social standing. I only got to hold you for a few minutes before they took you away from me. I have been tormented ever since that day." A tear rolled down Sadie's cheek.

Sienna could sense that Sadie was sincere. She got up from the table and walked over and gave Sadie a hug. Louanne then got up and walked over and gave them both a hug. The three women started to cry and then laugh together. Bill didn't know what to make of this. The four of them talked over supper and then Sienna, Louanne, and Sadie moved out onto the porch while Bill offered to clean up the kitchen and do the dishes. Bill later joined the women on the porch in time to hear Louanne say, "Then it is settled. You will stay here and help me run the Blue Dolphin." Bill didn't know what the conversation had been or how the ladies had come to this conclusion but he thought that this might be good for all of them. He thought to himself that he would never understand women and also if he would ever figure out what that second question was that Louanne said a guy should never answer.

The next couple of days, everyone spent time getting used to their new arrangements. It seemed that things were looking up for everyone. Sadie was staying sober. She had found her daughter. Louanne had a new friend and some extra help running the inn. Nathaniel had a permanent place to do his gardening maintenance. Bill and Sienna got to spend lots of time together. Bill thought this was just as Louanne had said the first day he met her. If something happened to you that seemed horrible and then takes you in a completely different path from what you wanted but then led you to something greater, was it really a bad thing that happened to you? Or was it a good thing? Bill thought that his getting dumped by Erica was now definitely a good thing because he had met and fell in love with Sienna.

But Jack and Erica hadn't really travelled that far. They were staying at a KOA campground near Santee, South Carolina. Jack was not about to walk away from all of that potential treasure, while Erica didn't fully understand what she was involved in. She thought that this was all about love and relationships. The couple had rented a trailer and as far as Erica was concerned, they were enjoying their summer break at this campground.

"Babe, I think I will head down to the recreation hall and see if there is anybody there to shoot some pool with," Jack told Erica. In reality, Jack was going stir crazy. He couldn't stop thinking about the treasure.

"Sure Babe, I'm just going get something ready for supper."

There were a couple of young guys playing pool inside the rec hall. One pool table wasn't in use and there was a fellow just watching the other young guys play. "Do you want to shoot a game?" Jack asked

"Sure, I'm not that good though."

"Me either."

"You break. My name is Jacques."

"Jock?"

"No Jacques. It's French Canadian. Just call me Jack. It's easier."

"Okay Jack. I'm Pete. I'm working here for the summer." Jack and Pete engaged in a game of spots and stripes. "So what brings y'all to Santee from Canada, Jack?"

"I quit medical school and it really ticked off my father. He is a quite well-off doctor in Montreal. My father was so mad at me that he disowned me. So I thought that I may as well travel around for the summer with my girlfriend and give him a chance to cool off."

"Yeah parents huh? What can you do? Say that's quite a ring you have on there."

"Thanks. My girlfriend gave it to me. She had it engraved JPF for Jacques Pierre Falstaff. I don't really care for it. Do you want to buy it?"

"No thanks. I can't afford something like that."

"Oh come on mate. Make me an offer."

"No thanks pal. I'm not interested."

"Well looks like you are going to beat me here Pete. All you need to do is sink the eight-ball."

"Good game Jack," Pete offered his condolences as he sunk the eight-ball.

"Pete, the office is closed for the night and I have to make an urgent phone call. Do you have a key to the office?"

"Yes, I do Jack. But there is a pay-phone near the showers."

"Yeah, I know, but I wanted a bit of privacy."

"Well, I guess I could let you in this one time."

Once inside the office, Pete waited near the door while Jack made his call.

"Hello Kitty," he said softly, "don't say my name. I don't want Fripp to know that you are talking to me. Is he near enough to hear or can you talk?"

"Fripp just stepped out," Kitty responded. "So I can talk Jack."

"So what's been happening?" Jack asked cunningly.

"There has been lots of excitement around here since you left Jack. Fripp and Bill and a bunch of other guys found a tunnel under the Alvermay that led over to the Old Exchange and Provost Dungeon. There was a skeleton down there and everything."

"You're right Kitty. That is exciting."

"I think one of the men died down there. But I'm not sure because Fripp isn't saying much."

"Did they find any treasure down there Kitty?"

"I don't think so. Fripp has been keeping close watch on a bunch of papers he said are from an old journal. He doesn't let them out of his sight. Then yesterday, he took them out to the Blue Dolphin Inn. He had them in an old civil war saddlebag."

"Thanks Kitty. You're a doll."

"What's this about Jack? I don't want to get in trouble with Fripp. Does this have something to do with that guy dying in the tunnel? Is that it? Oh my. Someone did die. Didn't they? Are you coming back here Jack?"

"Calm down Kitty. Everything is alright. Fripp and I just had a little bit of a disagreement. That's all. I was just calling to see if he had settled down. Yes I will be back. Everything will be fine. Nobody died."

"Oh I'm so glad Jack."

"Just don't tell Fripp that I called. I want it to be a surprise for him."

"Okay Jack. I won't tell him. Look after yourself. Are you still with that pretty girl who was here with you? Erin, or Elaine or something?"

"Erica. Yes, we're still hanging out together. Bye Kitty. Remember don't tell Fripp."

"Bye Jack."

"Sounds like you are involved in some secret agent type of stuff," Pete said as Jack hung up the phone.

"Nah, just some girl trouble."

"Oh I get it. That's why you didn't want to use the pay phone in case your girlfriend overheard you."

"You got it mate. Thanks for helping me out."

"No problem man. Anytime."

"Speaking of my girlfriend, she was making supper and I better get back to the trailer."

"Hey if you want to shoot some pool again tomorrow after my shift, just show up at the rec hall at the same time."

"I'll try," Jack answered.

Returning to the trailer, Jack asked, "Hey Babe, I just heard about this place down near Beaufort called the Blue Dolphin Inn. This guy said it is beautiful. Why don't we drive down there tomorrow and check it out?"

"That sounds great," Erica responded.

August 8th 1976

Walking into the Alvermay, a young man approached Fripp, "Hey man, do you have a room available to rent? I just need it for a couple of days."

"Sure. Room number three is vacant."

Kitty who was standing nearby jumped in, "That's Jack's room!"

"Jack's gone Kitty. He packed up and left. He's not coming back."

"I wouldn't be so sure about that Fripp."

"Why do you say that, Kitty? Has Jack been here?"

"No he hasn't. He called but I'm not supposed to tell you. He said that the two of you had a falling out and he wanted to make it up to you as a surprise. Did I do something wrong?"

"It's okay Kitty. What did he say?"

"He was asking about treasure. I told him that you found a tunnel under the Alvermay and that you took some papers out to the Blue Dolphin Inn."

"Oh no!" Fripp grabbed the phone and started dialing the Blue Dolphin Inn. The phone kept ringing and ringing with no answer. "Kitty, I'm going out to the Blue Dolphin to make sure that everything is okay. You look after the Alvermay for me please."

Kitty was panicking. "What's wrong Fripp? What's happening? Is this my fault? I was only trying to help you and Jack make amends with each other."

"Kitty, calm down. I will call you later. Just look after things here for me. I'm not sure exactly when I'll be back."

SUMTER COUNTY

SOUTH CAROLINA

AUGUST 1976

Fripp arrived at the Blue Dolphin Inn and threw the door open. He called out in a panic, "Louanne! Sienna! Bill!" There was no answer. He raced from cabin to cabin searching. As he entered cabin number three, he found Sienna, Bill, Sadie, and Nathaniel Brown. They were tied up and gagged.

"Where's mom?" he frantically asked as he untied first Sienna and then Bill.

"They took her."

"Where were they heading?"

"I suspect they are heading to Williamsburg," Bill answered. "I told them that we had figured out that the treasure was hidden in the powder magazine. We didn't think they would take Louanne hostage. They also took the saddle bag with all of our research and the papers that you brought the other day."

"That's the least of my concerns," Fripp responded. "Louanne has diabetes and needs her medication or she could go into a coma. Let's get going. We'll catch them. That Volkswagen is no match for my Camaro. Sienna, you grab mom's medication from the house and I will pick you up at the front door."

Fripp took every Lowcountry short cut that he knew of as he raced northward towards Virginia. On Interstate 95 just north of Highway 26, Bill spotted an orange Volkswagen sitting at a truck stop. Fripp pulled into the truck stop but parked a distance away from the Volkswagen. Bill got out of the Camaro and made his way up to the restaurant window. He could see Erica and Jack sitting at a table inside, eating fruit and ice cream. Knowing that they were busy, Bill then went to the Volkswagen. He could see Louanne lying in the back seat. She was bound and gagged. Bill opened the door to get Louanne out but her body was lifeless. She had died of a diabetic seizure.

Bill reluctantly went back over to the Camaro and broke the news to Fripp and Sienna. Sienna burst into tears. Fripp though, was overcome with a different emotion. Bill could see seething anger in his eyes.

Fripp got out of the car and went to the trunk. "Come here Bill," Fripp directed showing Bill the George Washington rifle in the trunk. He then took an object wrapped in old linen cloth from the trunk and handed it to Bill.

"What is it Fripp," Bill asked as he unwrapped the object.

"I believe that is the Holy Grail. I found it along with the missing pages from Robert Keith Dick's journal when I opened the first barrel that we found in the cistern on Glebe Street. I was going to keep it. I'm sorry son, that I was hiding it from you."

"But how do you know Fripp?"

"I didn't show you all of the missing pages. According to one page, Robert Keith hid the grail in the barrel to protect it from the British so they couldn't take it back to England with them when they left Charleston. You keep these, son. Here are the keys to the Camaro. Take Sienna and go north back to Canada. Please, look after my baby girl, Bill. Treat her good." Fripp closed the trunk and went to the glove box. He took out some ammunition and then reached under the passenger seat for a .357 Magnum pistol, "I have some business to finish with Jack."

Fripp hugged his teary-eyed daughter goodbye and then went over to the orange Volkswagen and climbed into the back seat. Bill had a brief thought to stop Fripp, to talk him out of what he was about to do, but at that point, Sienna's safety was the most important thing to him. And though he didn't believe in vengeance, he felt that it was not his place to stop him. It was between Fripp and Jack, and Fripp and God. Bill and Sienna got into the Camaro and headed north on Interstate 95, never looking back.

"Hey man. Was that you and your girlfriend driving that orange bug?" a young trucker asked approaching Jack and Erica.

"Yeah. What's it to ya?" Jack responded indignantly.

"Hey pal, don't get upset with me. I was just going to tell you that I saw a fellow climbing into the back seat and it looked like he was carrying a gun."

"Sorry man. Thanks for the heads up. Was he a white guy about 20 years old, 5' 5" or so?"

"No man. This was a black guy about 40 years old or so," the trucker explained.

"Fripp?" Erica asked.

"Yeah Fripp. Hey pal let us buy you some fruit and ice cream to thank you," Jack offered.

Sensing that they seemed like okay couple, the trucker sat down with Jack and Erica, "So, who is this Fripp guy?"

"Erica and I stayed at his hotel in Charleston. He thinks we still owe him some money. He doesn't mean us any harm. Fripp is just looking to scare us a little."

Erica didn't say anything. She didn't know what to think of the situation anymore. Erica knew that Jack and her had Louanne tied up in the back seat but she still didn't know what was on Jack's mind.

"Hey buddy," Jack said. "Do you want to help us get back at him? Nothing serious. Just shake him up a bit."

"I'm not sure. What do you have in mind? I told you that I thought I saw him with a gun," the trucker expressed with great hesitation in his voice.

"Well you are about the same size and build as me. You look about my age and even have some of my features. How about if we change clothes and you go to my car pretending to be me?"

"Are you crazy? How do I know he doesn't want to shoot me? I mean you." The trucker started to get up from the table.

"Wait!" Jack said. "I will pay you."

"How much?"

"A hundred bucks."

"A hundred bucks and your watch."

"Done."

Jack and the trucker went into the washroom and after another man had left, they exchanged clothes. "You don't happen to have a gun in your truck do you?" Jack asked the trucker.

"Well, yes I do but you said there wasn't going to be any trouble. You said this Fripp guy just wanted to scare you."

"I just want to use it to catch him off guard. Sort of balance things out and disarm him."

"There's a small pistol in my glove box."

Back out in the restaurant area, Jack explained his plan to Erica and the trucker, "You two get into the car and make sure that you don't let Fripp see your face. He will likely point his gun at you which probably isn't even loaded, and tell you to drive somewhere. I will sneak up on Erica's side of the car with your gun and point it at Fripp to disarm him. Then you can be on your way with your hundred bucks and my watch."

"That sounds simple enough," the trucker agreed.

Erica and the trucker walked toward the Volkswagen as Jack went to the truckers rig and took the pistol from the glove box.

Inside the Volkswagen, Fripp pointed his gun to the back of the trucker's head thinking that it was Jack, "You've really made a mess of things Jack. You've killed my wife! My life is ruined because of you!"

"We didn't kill her Fripp!" Erica cried. "She just died, honest."

"Shut up girl! You're an accomplice now."

The trucker was now becoming very concerned. There seemed to be a lot more involved than what Jack had let on. Just as he turned to face Fripp to explain that he wasn't Jack, Jack appeared at the passenger's window and shoved the trucker's pistol right through the window. Fripp was still looking toward the trucker trying to figure out what was going on when Jack pulled the trigger hitting Fripp in the chest. People walking through the parking lot looked up momentarily and then assumed that the noise was just a truck backfiring.

"Jack! What are you doing?" Erica exclaimed.

"Never mind. We are all going to leave in this fellow's truck. Now move it. Get out of the car and walk towards the truck. Don't try anything man or I'll drop you just like I dropped my friend Fripp." Jack grabbed the gun from Fripp's limp body but in his haste, he forgot the saddle bag.

Jack, Erica, and the trucker climbed into the truckers rig with the trucker driving and Jack and Erica beside him. "Head north on Interstate 95," Jack demanded. After travelling a little bit north, Jack instructed the trucker to exit near Locklair Road. Just off the Interstate, Jack told the trucker to pull over.

"C'mon the two of you get out here!"

"Jack, what are you doing? You aren't going to leave us here are you?"

"Just get out Erica. You are now a liability to me."

"I thought you loved me Jack!"

"If you wanted someone to love you, you should have stayed with that wimp Bill. He loved you. I only needed you so I could learn about the treasure from him," Jack said as he shoved Erica and the trucker toward the ditch.

"Give me your wallet and your identification," Jack commanded of the trucker. "Here is that watch you wanted. Put it on. Put my ring on too."

"I gave you that ring as a gift Jack. It has your initials engraved," Erica pleaded.

"It won't matter anymore Erica. Both of you kneel down now!"

Erica and the trucker knelt alongside the ditch. Erica was crying and pleading, "Please Jack, don't do this!"

Jack squeezed the trigger of the .357 Magnum twice, hitting Erica and the trucker in the back. They slumped to the ground and then rolling them over, he shot them each again in the neck and chest. Jack spent the night sleeping in the cab of the rig and then early the next morning, on August 9th, reported to the police that he had found the bodies on the side of the road when he pulled over to rest.

Sienna was devastated over her mother. She couldn't control her sobs. She sat in the passenger seat, her body shaking as she cried.

"I'm so sorry Sienna. It's all my fault. I'm so sorry I brought all this on you."

"It's not your fault Bill," she whimpered. "I love you, I don't blame you."

"I know you're hurting right now. But I am going to spend our whole lives trying to make you happy. You deserve the world."

"I don't want the world Bill. I just want you."

He reached over and took her hand in his, squeezing it tight.

That one simple touch soothed some of her pain. She knew he would look after her from now on. She knew things would be ok one day. She needed to grieve over losing her mother, and she would, but she knew she needed to be strong right now. She wiped the wetness from her cheeks.

"Where are we going to go?"

"We are going to go to Canada. I just have to make a stop in Williamsburg first."

"As far as . . . goody, I've never been to Williamsburg," Nathaniel said excitedly from the backseat of the Camaro.

With moist eyes, Sienna smiled at Nathaniel's innocence, knowing that he didn't understand the gravity of what was happening.

Bill entered the Pasteur and Galt Apothecary Shop followed by Sienna and then Nathaniel. The front door of the building opened into a large open room with a long counter along the left side. Against the wall, behind the counter, was a bank of drawers with shelves above. They extended the entire length of the wall. The shelves were filled with jars and containers that held creams, medicinal herbs, spices, and elixirs that would have been used in the eighteenth century. A woman in period costume was describing to a tour group, how the various cures would have been used in the eighteenth century. The woman motioned for the tour group to go into the back room where Dr. Pasteur and Dr. Galt would carry on examinations and surgeries if necessary.

Bill stayed back a little to allow others to enter the interior room ahead of him. In this way he was at the back of the crowd and in part still in the main room. From under his jacket which was draped over his arm, Bill pulled out the old linen cloth and unwrapped the Holy Grail. He stepped in behind the counter and set the Grail on the top shelf among the other containers. Bill smiled at it then turned to join the tour group once again. Sienna was unaware of what he had just done.

Bill, Sienna, and Nathaniel next went into the Raleigh Tavern. While Sienna and Nathaniel explored the various rooms, Bill combed the guest registrar. He found the name Zachary Owens registered as a guest from 1771 until 1776. In one way he thought this was impossible. In another way it proved B.S. Jack's story all the more so. It's true, Bill thought. The treasure is out there somewhere and I am about to walk away from it all.

Sienna walked up behind him and putting her hand on his shoulder reasoned, "We should get going if you've seen everything that you want to see here in Williamsburg."

Looking into her eyes and gazing upon her face, Bill knew that they were going to have a wonderful life together and that she was worth more than all the silver and gold that his ancestors had protected for so long and then sent over from Scotland to the colonies. He took her in his arms and kissed her. "Let's go. It's time we leave the past behind," Bill said to Sienna, but more so to convince himself.

The next day, on August 10th, 1976 as Bill, Sienna, and Nathaniel Brown left Williamsburg for Canada, a news bulletin came over the radio, reporting that the day before, on August 9th, a truck driver had found the bodies of a young man and a young woman on Locklair Road just off Interstate 95 near Road 341. They had been shot with a .357 Magnum. Apparently, the woman was 5' 5" and the man was 6' 1". Both were about 20 years old. The woman was wearing cut-off blue jeans and a pink halter top. The man was wearing faded Levi blue jeans and a red t-shirt with Coors America's light beer on the front. It was announced on the radio that there was no identification on the bodies and if anyone could provide any information to please contact Teddy Manns at the Sumter County Sheriff's Office 803-436-2790.

Bill and Sienna looked at each other knowing that this had to be Jack Falstaff and Erica that the news report was referring to. Further they knew that Fripp had to be the shooter. Bill thought that Jack Falstaff got what was coming to him but he couldn't help but feel sadness that Erica had been killed.

When they reached the Buffalo/Fort Erie border crossing, the crossing guard asked to see some identification. "So Zachary Owens," he questioned, "is this your car?"

"No sir. It's her father's car. She's my fiancé."

"Is that right miss?"

"Yes sir," Sienna responded proudly as she took hold of Bill's hand.

"And you in the back seat. Who are you?"

"As Far As, I know I am the best man."

The guard smiled, "Well have a nice wedding you two. Carry on Zachary Owens."

As they drove away, Sienna turned to Bill with the sweetest smile on her face and said,

"Well, I guess I should start calling you Zach."

WHEN HORSES LIE DOWN

2010

"Papa, that's quite a story. Is it true?" I asked.

"Not a word of it Sunshine, not a single word."

"Paaapaaa, you're teasing me. Some of it has to be true. It sounds like it could be."

"Zachary Owens, leave the girl alone," Wee Nanny piped up.

"Well that's my story and I'm sticking to it," Papa said unapologetically, while picking his tea up again and taking another sip.

I made it through my first year at McMaster, regrets and all. But the week before I was set to head back to school for my second year, Papa became very ill. I made a decision not to go back, but instead, to move back in with my Papa and Granny Sienna. My Papa objected, arguing that I would one day regret this, and that he didn't want to be the cause of anyone's regrets, especially not mine. But something deep down told me that I'd regret it more if I didn't. He eventually settled into the idea, and stopped telling me to go back to school and quit wasting my time on an old man. He was enjoying my presence around the house again—afternoon chats, tea on the front porch at night, just like when I was younger. Having me back home was probably the best medicine he could have, my Granny Sienna told me. And it was a great help to her too, me taking Papa to all his doctors' appointments, so she could care for As Far As and tend to things around the house.

The doctors were having a difficult time trying to diagnose his illness. Papa still kept trying to tell me stories to teach me lessons but I had heard most of them over and over again. By late fall, his condition had worsened. The doctors weren't saying it, but it was clear the situation was hopeless. He stayed in bed most days; any energy he had left was diminishing. They said it was time for him to stay at the hospital; he refused, just like Wee Nanny and I knew he would. But finally he was ready—I think he was ready in more ways than that.

On his last night at home, I went into his bedroom to see him. The room was dark, yet I could still see his eyes light up when he saw me. "Do you need anything Papa?" I asked.

"No, I'm okay. Thank you." He pointed to the wall, "Look Carolina." He chuckled to himself. I looked up to see the Quiet Light appear and then disappear. "Do you remember Carolina?"

"I will never forget Papa."

Then he started to chuckle. "What is it Papa?" I asked.

"It just occurred to me what the second question was that Granny Sienna's mother, Louanne, said you never answer if your wife or girlfriend asks you."

"What is it?

"Does this outfit make me look fat?"

Across the field from my Papa's house was a horse breeder and riding stable. When I was a little girl, I used to walk across the field and stand in the warm summer sun with my nose pressed to the fence watching these beautiful animals prancing around the field. It was exciting watching these magnificent creatures at play. They would come over to the fence and I would pet them. Their coats were so soft to touch and I loved the smell of them. They got to know that I always carried treats so when they would see me coming, the horses would quickly make their way to the fence. One day as we were driving by, I noticed that some of them were lying down. "Papa," I asked. "Why are those horses lying down? My friend at school said that horses only lie down when they are sick and if they lie down they're going to die."

"Horses usually sleep standing up because they are prey to other animals and if they are lying down they are more vulnerable," he replied. "They have a way of locking their legs so that they can sleep standing up without falling over."

"Then why are those ones lying down?"

"Sometimes they just want to lie down to rest. If there are other horses standing around to keep watch over them then they feel safe and are comfortable enough to lie down and go to sleep."

My Papa passed away that night. He was there and then he wasn't, just like the Quiet Light. As Far As was inconsolable, Granny Sienna was strong like she always was, I was lost. He was gone, and so was his wisdom and guidance. But Granny Sienna saw it another way.

"Your Papa saw to it that you were carefully taught, Carolina. That will stay with you always. Everything you need to know is already up there," she said patting my head, "and there." She pointed to my heart.

In the weeks that followed, Keegan and I rekindled our relationship. He was home from McMaster for winter break and proved to be a real support to Granny Sienna and I while we went through this despairing time. Having him around again, feeling such love and kindness, reminded me of why I had loved him before and stirred in me a new love and respect for him.

I stayed at the house still with Wee Nanny, even though she protested. She said I had spent enough time putting my own life on hold. But I wasn't quite ready to move on, and start a new life yet.

One evening was particularly cold so Wee Nanny started a fire. We sat and chatted, enjoying the warmth from the fire. There is no heat like the heat of a wood fire. The odor of the burning wood and crackling sound is so relaxing.

"Your Papa used to love sitting here by the fire and listening to his old record albums."

"I can picture him doing that, sitting here, looking at his civil war stuff, listening to his music, admiring his old rifle."

"Yes, Carolina, he loved that old rifle. He brought it with him when we came from the United States."

"Hmm, I wonder," I said softly as I got up and lifted the rifle from its resting place, hanging on the mantle. I looked at the back and read, "*To my friend Alexander Dick—Shoot Straight. Ben Franklin.*"

"Pardon."

I repeated, "*To my friend Alexander Dick—Shoot Straight. Ben Franklin.*"

"Well, your Papa always said that old gun had some history."

"Wait a minute," I walked to the entrance where Papa had hung up that old, brown saddle bag. I brought it back to the family room and dumped the contents onto the coffee table. There were drawings and notes. There were brochures and maps that were marked up with pens and markers. I recalled that day that Mr. Fripp had called at my Papa's door and said that he had found all of it. Did he mean that he had found all of the Dick family treasure? Or was he referring to the Templar's Treasure? I wondered. Did these maps and notes point to the locations where Mr. Fripp said that he re-hid everything? I was growing excited. My sense of adventure was piquing in me.

I decided to do some research into many of the things that my Papa told me about. One advantage that I now had was the internet and my laptop computer. Looking on the internet, I checked out murders in South Carolina in 1976. There was an unsolved case involving a man and woman in their early twenties. The police report said that they had been shot with a .357 Magnum. The couple had been found on Locklair Road, between Interstate 95 and South Carolina 341 in Sumter County. The man and woman could not be identified but the man was wearing a ring with the initials JPF engraved into it. Jack Pierre Falstaff and Erica, I thought. Could it possibly be? The report went on to say that prior to their murder, it appears that they had been eating fruit and ice cream.

One report on the internet said that a fellow, from a KOA campground in Santee, South Carolina, claimed to have met a person called Jacques who called himself Jack.

Next, I looked up Dr. Alexander Dick. Sure enough, my research found that Dr. Alexander Dick once owned Prestonfield House in Edinburgh, Scotland and apparently a regular visitor of his was Benjamin Franklin.

And what of William Dick? This too proved to be true. I found that he apparently had been the richest man in Scotland and was thrown into prison by Cromwell. Was this actually my own ancestor?

I decided that I had to go to Charleston. I had to see all the things my Papa had told me about for myself. I was finally ready to set out on my own. Granny Sienna was sad to see me go, but encouraging. Keegan wasn't happy to be losing me again.

By the time they were my age, both my mother and Wee Nanny were already married. It wasn't that I didn't love Keegan or want to spend my life with him. It was just that my Papa had inspired in me a sense of adventure. And an adventure was calling. Keegan understood. And I knew, as my Papa used to tell me, if it was meant to be then it'll be.

I left for Charleston in the summer, after much planning and preparation. Upon arriving, I went and sat on the cistern at the College of Charleston in front of Randolph Hall. It was as my Papa described it. I walked down to 6 Glebe Street and stood there looking, trying to picture my Papa, Fripp, Granny Sienna, and the Thompson twins digging up the cistern. Then I made my way over to 35 Meeting Street. It was magnificent.

Taking the tour of the Edmondston-Alston House, it too was how my Papa described. As we toured into the dining room, the tour guide pointed out a silver candlestick that was missing its mate. Didn't my Papa tell me in his story that Jack Falstaff had stolen a silver candlestick? This was way too weird. When the tour guide started her tour going toward the second floor, she said, "Be careful of the first step as it is a different height than the others and many people almost trip on it." Pausing on the step, I was awed. This is exactly where my Papa and Fripp almost fell when they were running away after Jack stole the rifle.

I walked up East Battery to 120 East Bay Street. I stood in front of what was now a liquor store. Inside, the clerk asked if she could help me with anything but how could I possibly begin to explain why I was there. Looking around, I tried to picture the bar and the tables the way my Papa told me.

After spending the night in a local hotel, I went down to Beaufort and sat in the park on the waterfront. I grabbed a coffee as my Papa had done and sat there thinking about him sitting, watching T.W. Wolfe search through the garbage cans and Nathaniel Brown cleaning up the park for a dollar that my Papa would have to pay in advance. And what about Sadie? Asking around, I found that the Blue Dolphin Inn had long closed its doors when the owner, Sadie, had passed away.

After giving it much thought, I decided that I was going to search out the treasure using the documents that Fripp left with my Papa. Don't get the wrong idea. I did learn from my Papa that happiness doesn't come from having lots of money. I was 'carefully taught' so to speak. I planned to find the treasure and use it to help those in need. That's what my Papa would do, and that's what he would want me to do.

I needed to go back home to Grand Valley, Ontario to regroup and see where I was going to start my journey of search. Plus, I wanted to talk my younger brother into working with me on this. He is a great outdoorsman and very smart when it comes to looking at maps and things. But before I returned home, there was one place left that I thought I should visit. That place of course was where this story started with Benjamin Franklin, George Washington, and Thomas Jefferson, in Williamsburg, Virginia.

I walked into the Raleigh Tavern. It was exactly how Papa had described it when he told me his story. Upon entering a small room off the main room, I stood in awe wondering to myself if this could possibly be the room that Benjamin Franklin, George Washington, and Thomas Jefferson first discussed getting funding from Dr. Alexander Dick to finance the Revolutionary War. Was I standing in the exact room?

Back out by the bar, I asked a costumed period interpreter if there were any guest registers from 1771.

"Any documents from that time period are secured away in the library. We do have a reproduction that you could look at though. It is at the end of the bar."

"Thank you," I said as I whisked my way to the end of the bar and began combing through the register book. "Owens. Owens," I repeated flipping through the pages. "Owens." There it was! Zachary Owens was registered as a guest on October 20th, 1771. Was my Papa telling me the truth about his experience in Charleston and about the Templar's treasure and the Dick family fortune? There was one more thing I needed to check out before I could conclude that it was all true.

It was just a short walk down Duke of Gloucester Street to the Apothecary of Dr. Galt and Dr. Pasteur. As I entered the front door of the building, a woman in period costume was describing to a tour group various cures that were used in the eighteenth century. She stood behind a long counter that was along the left side of the room. Against the wall, behind the counter, was a bank of drawers with shelves above. They extended the entire length of the wall. The shelves were filled with jars and containers that held creams, medicinal herbs, spices, and elixirs. I asked her about the pewter chalice on the shelf in the upper right corner.

"I am afraid that we don't really know much about that artifact," she said. "We believe that it is possible that it could be two thousand years old. We are not sure why it is here with Dr. Pasteur's and Dr. Galt's remedies and equipment."

Boldly, I asked, "Could I hold it?"

"I'm sorry dear, we have a no touching policy."

I must have had a really disappointed look on my face because a moment later as she took the group into the examination and surgery room, she turned to me and said, "Oh, I guess it wouldn't hurt just this once." She reached up and took the chalice from the shelf. As the woman handed it to me, a blue, crumpled piece of paper fell out onto the floor. "Look at that," the woman expressed with disgust, "someone has put their garbage in here." Unfolding the paper, she mumbled, "How about that. It is an old driver's licence from Ontario, Canada from 1976 belonging to a William Dick. Interesting," she surmised as she crumpled the paper back up and tossed it in a garbage can behind the counter. "Here you go dear," the woman said as she passed the chalice to me.

I wondered, was I holding the Holy Grail? Is this the actual cup that Jesus Christ used at the last supper? Is this the chalice that in my Papa's story, came from the barrel in the cistern in Charleston and he placed here at the Apothecary? Does this mean that stories of the Templar's Treasure are true? Does this mean that some of the Dick family fortune is still hidden out there? Did Fripp actually find it all and now I have all of the documents in my car that will lead me to all of the treasure?

Thoughts were running through my mind so fast it was making my head spin. I held the cup up to the light and looked it over, up and down, inside and out. I didn't want to give it back ever.

Suddenly, I felt a squeezing pain in my upper, left arm and I heard a voice from behind "I'm Jack Falstaff. I believe that you have something that belongs to me."

Thus my story begins.